House of Thieves

House of Thieves

KAUI HART HEMMINGS

The Penguin Press

New York

2005

THE PENGUIN PRESS
Published by the Penguin Group
Penguin Group (USA) Inc., 375 Hudson Street, New York, New York 10014, U.S.A. •
Penguin Group (Canada), 10 Alcorn Avenue, Toronto, Ontario, Canada M4V 3B2
(a division of Pearson Penguin Canada Inc.) • Penguin Books Ltd, 80 Strand, London
WC2R 0RL, England • Penguin Ireland, 25 St. Stephen's Green, Dublin 2, Ireland
(a division of Penguin Books Ltd) • Penguin Books Australia Ltd, 250 Camberwell Road,
Camberwell, Victoria 3124, Australia (a division of Pearson Australia Group Pty Ltd) •
Penguin Books India Pvt Ltd, 11 Community Centre, Panchsheel Park, New Delhi –
110 017, India • Penguin Group (NZ), Cnr Airborne and Rosedale Roads, Albany,
Auckland 1310, New Zealand (a division of Pearson New Zealand Ltd) • Penguin Books
(South Africa) (Pty) Ltd, 24 Sturdee Avenue, Rosebank, Johannesburg 2196, South Africa •
Penguin Books Ltd, Registered Offices: 80 Strand, London WC2R 0RL, England

First published in 2005 by The Penguin Press, a member of Penguin Group (USA) Inc.

"House of Thieves" (as "Outlaw Ride") first appeared in *Zoetrope: All-Story.* "The Minor
Wars" first appeared in *StoryQuarterly* and later in *Falling Backwards: Stories of Fathers
and Daughters,* edited by Gina Frangello (Hourglass Books) and *The Best American Nonrequired Reading,* edited by Dave Eggers (Houghton Mifflin).

Grateful acknowledgment is made for permission to use illustrations and an excerpt from
Get Tough! How to Win in Hand-to-Hand Fighting by W. E. Fairbairn. By permission of
A. P. Watt Ltd on behalf of Devon & Cornwall Constabulary Compassionate Fund and Lyn
Fairbairn.

PUBLISHER'S NOTE
These selections are works of fiction. Names, characters, places, and incidents either are the
product of the author's imagination or are used fictitiously, and any resemblance to actual
persons, living or dead, business establishments, events, or locales is entirely coincidental.

LIBRARY OF CONGRESS CATALOGING IN PUBLICATION DATA
Hemmings, Kaui Hart.
House of thieves / Kaui Hart Hemmings.
p. cm.
Contents: The minor wars—Final girl—House of thieves—Island cowboys—Begin
with an outline—Secret clutch—Ancient weapons—Location scouts—The after party.
ISBN 1-59420-048-3
1. Hawaii—Social life and customs—Fiction. 2. Upper class families—Fiction.
3. Teenagers—Fiction. I. Title.
PS3608.E477H68 2005
813'.6—dc22   2004065947

This book is printed on acid-free paper. ∞

Printed in the United States of America
1 3 5 7 9 10 8 6 4 2

Designed by Chris Welch

For Andy and Eleanor

Contents

House of Thieves

The Minor Wars

The sun is shining, mynah birds are hopping, palm trees are swaying, so what. I sit down in my easy chair. I've brought it here from home. I pick up the spoon from my lunch tray. I'd like to fling this spoon into the air, catch it in my mouth, and say, "Look at that, Boots." Boots is my wife, although I haven't called her that since the early seventies when she used to wear these orange knee-high boots in eighty-six-degree weather. She'd top my utensil act by using a fork or a steak knife. Her real name is Joanie, and she's barefoot. She's in a coma. Dying the slowest of deaths. Or perhaps I'm wrong. Perhaps she has never felt more alive.

"Shut this crap off," I tell Scottie, my ten-year-old daughter. Her real name is Scottie. She turns off the television with the remote.

"No, I mean this." I point to the stuff in the window—the sun and the trees.

Scottie slides the curtain across the window, shutting all of it out. "This curtain is sure heavy," she says.

She needs a haircut or a brushing. There are small tumbleweeds of hair rolling over the back of her head. She is one of those kids who always seem to need a haircut. I'm grateful that she isn't pretty, but I realize this could change.

"It's like the bib I have to wear at the dentist when he needs X-rays of my gums." She knocks on the hard curtain. "I wish we were at the dentist."

"Me, too," I say, and it's true. A root canal would be a blast compared to this. Life has been strange without Joanie's voice commanding it. I have to cook now and clean and give Scottie orders. That's been weird. I've never been that full-time parent, supervising the children on weekdays, setting schedules and boundaries. Now I see Scottie before school and right after school, and I'm basically with her until she goes to bed. She's a funny kid.

The visitor on my wife's bed looks at Scottie standing by the shaded window and frowns, then turns on a light with a remote control and goes back to work on Joanie's face. My wife is in a coma and this woman is applying makeup to her lips. I have to admit that Joanie would appreciate this. She enjoys being beautiful, and she likes to look good whether she's canoeing across the Molokai channel or getting tossed from an offshore powerboat.

She likes to look *luminous* and *ravishing*—her own words. Good luck, I always tell her. Good luck with your goals. I don't love my wife as I'm supposed to, but I love her in my own way. To my knowledge, she doesn't adore me either, but we are content with our individual schedules and our lives together, and are quite proud of our odd system.

We tried for a while to love each other normally, urged by her brother to subject ourselves to counseling as a decent couple would. Barry, her brother, is a man of the couch, a believer in therapy, affirmations, and pulse points. Once, he tried to show us exercises he'd been doing in session with his new woman friend. We were instructed to trade reasons, abstract or specific, why we stayed with one another. I started off by saying that she would get really drunk and pretend I was someone else and do this really neat thing with her tongue. Joanie said tax breaks. Barry cried. Openly. Joanie and Barry's parents are divorced and his second wife had recently left him for a man who understood that a man didn't do volunteer work. Barry wanted us to reflect on bonds and promises and love and such. He was tired of things breaking apart. Tired of people resigning so easily. We tried for Barry, but our marriage only seemed to work when we didn't try at all.

The lady with the makeup (Tia? Tara? Someone who models with Joanie) has stopped her dabbing and is looking at Scottie. The light is hitting this woman's face, giving me the opportunity to see that she should perhaps be working on her own makeup. The color of her face, a manila envelope. Specks of white in her eyebrows. Concealer not concealing. I can tell my daughter doesn't know what to do with this stare.

"What?" Scottie asks.

"I think your mother was enjoying the view," Tia, or Tara, says.

I jump in to protect my daughter, who is silent and confused.

"Listen here, T. Her mother was not enjoying the view. Her mother is in a coma."

"My name is not T," T says. "My name is Allison."

"Okay then, listen here, Ali. Don't confuse my daughter."

"I'm turning into a remarkable young lady," Scottie says.

"Damn straight," I say.

This Ali person gets back to business. Scottie turns the television back on. Another dating show. I'm running out of toys. I can usually find a toy in anything. A spoon, a sugar packet, a quarter. Our first week here, I made up this game: who could get the most slices of banana stuck to the ceiling. You had to put a piece on a napkin and then try to trampoline it up there. Scottie loved it. Nurses got involved. Even the neurologist gave it a go. But now we're nearing the end of our fourth week here and I'm running out of tricks. The neurologist says her scores are lower on the various coma scales. She says things, uses language I don't understand, and yet I understand her—I know what she's telling me.

"Last time you were the one on the bed," Scottie says.

"Yup."

"Last time you lied to me."

"I know, Scottie. Forgive me." My motorcycling accident. At home I insisted I was okay, that I wasn't going to go to the hospital. Scottie issued me these little tests to demonstrate my unreliability. Joanie participated. They played bad cop, worse cop.

"How many fingers?" Scottie asked, holding up what I thought was a pinky and a thumb: a shaka.

"Balls," I said. I didn't want to be tested this way.

"Answer her," Joanie said.

"Two?"

"Okay," Scottie said warily. "Close your eyes and touch your nose and stand on one foot."

"Balls, Scottie. I can't do that regardless, and you're treating me like a drunk driver."

"Do what she says," Joanie yelled.

I stood still in protest. I knew something was wrong with me, but I didn't want to go to the hospital. I wanted to let what was wrong with my body run its course. I was curious. I was having trouble holding up my head.

"Look at yourself," Joanie said. "You can't even see straight."

"How am I supposed to look at myself, then?"

Turns out I had damaged my fourth nerve, a nerve

that connects your eyes to your brain, which explained why things had been out of focus.

"You could have died," Scottie says. She's watching Allison brush color onto Joanie's cheeks.

"No way," I say. "A fourth nerve? Who needs it?"

"You lied. You said you were okay. You said you could see my fingers."

"I didn't lie. I guessed correctly. Plus, for a while there I got to have twins. Two Scotties."

Scottie nods. "Well. Okay."

I remember when I was in the hospital Joanie put vodka into my Jell-O. She wore my eye patch and teased me and stayed with me. It was very nice. I'm wondering what my accident has to do with anything. Lately, Scottie's been pointing out my flaws, my tricks and lies. She's interviewing me. I'm the backup candidate. I'm the dad.

Scottie touches her mother's hair. It's slippery-looking. It looks the way it did when she gave birth to Scottie and our other daughter, Alexandra. Allison is now looking at me as if I'm disturbed. "You have an odd way of speaking to children," she says.

"Parents shouldn't have to compromise their personalities," Scottie says.

It's something I've heard Joanie tell our other daughter. I catch a glimpse of my wife's face. She looks so lovely. Not ravishing, but simply lovely. Her freckles rising through the blush, her closed eyes fastened by dark, dramatic lashes. These lashes are the only strong feature left on her face. Everything has been softened. She looks pretty, but perhaps too divine; too bone china white, as if she's underwater or cased in glass. Oddly, the effect makes me like all the things I usually don't like about her. I like that she forgets to wash the lettuce and our salads are always pebbly. Or sometimes we go to this restaurant that's touristy, but the fish is great, and without fail she ends up at the bar with these Floridian spring-break sorts for a drink or ten and I'm left at the table all alone. I usually don't enjoy this, but now I don't mind so much. I like her magnetism. I like her courage and ego. But maybe I only like these things because she may not wake up again. It's confusing.

The manager of that restaurant once thanked me. He said that she always livened up the place and made people want to drink. I'm sure if she died, he'd put her picture up because it's that kind of restaurant— pictures of local legends and dead patrons haunting the walls. I feel sad that she has to die for her picture to go up on the wall, or for me to really love everything about her.

"Allison," I say. "Thank you. I'm sure Joanie is so pleased."

"She's not pleased. She's in a coma," Allison says.

I'm speechless.

"Oh my God," Allison says, and she starts to cry. "I can't believe I said that. I was just trying to sound like you. To get you back."

She leaves the room with her beauty tools.

"Oh, mercy. I need to change some habits. I'm an ass," I say.

"You're my dad," Scottie says.

"Yes," I say. "Yes."

"You're a dad-ass. Like a bad-ass but older."

"Mercy," I say.

Scottie wants me to step into the waiting room with her. She has something to tell me. This is routine. She's afraid of speaking to her mother. She's embarrassed of her life. A ten-year-old, worried that her life isn't interesting enough. She thinks that if she speaks to her mother, she should have something incredible to say. I always urge her to talk about school or the dogs, but Scottie says that this would be boring, and she wouldn't want her mother to think she was a walking yawn. For the past few weeks or so, Scottie has been trying to have these worthy experiences after school at the beach club.

"Okay, Scottie," I say. "Today's the day. You're going to talk to Mom. You can read an article, you can sing a song, or tell her what you learned in school. Right-o?"

"Okay, but I have a story."

"Talk to me."

She smiles. "Okay, pretend you're Mom," she says. "Close your eyes."

I close my eyes.

"Hi, Mom. Yesterday I explored the reef in front of the public beach by myself. I have tons of friends, but I felt like being alone. There's this really cute guy who works the beach stand there. His eyes look like giraffe eyes."

I'm trying not to smile.

"The tide was low. I could see all sorts of things. In one place the coral was a really cool dark color, but then I looked closer and it wasn't the coral. It was an eel. A moray. I almost died. There were millions of sea urchins and a few sea cucumbers. I even picked one up and squeezed him."

"This is good, Scottie. Let's go back in. Mom will love this."

"I'm not done."

"Oh." I close my eyes again.

"I was squatting on the reef and lost my balance and fell back on my hands. One of my hands landed on an urchin and it put its spines in me. My hand looked like a pincushion."

I'm grabbing her hands, holding them up to my face. The roots of urchin spines are locked in and expanded under the skin of her left palm. They look like tiny black starfish that plan on making this hand their home forever. I notice more stars on her fingertips. "Why didn't you tell me you were hurt? Why didn't you say something?"

"I'm okay. I handled it. I didn't really fall."

"What do you mean? Are these pen marks?"

"Yes."

I look closer. I feel her palm and press on the marks.

"Ow," she says, and pulls her hand back. "Just kidding," she says. "They're real. But I didn't really fall. I did it on purpose. I slammed my hand into an urchin. But I'm not telling Mom that part."

"What?" I can't imagine Scottie feeling such terrible pain. "Why would you do this? Scottie?"

"For a story, I guess."

"But Christ, didn't it hurt?"

"Yes."

"Balls, Scottie. I'm floored right now. Completely floored."

"Do you want to hear the rest?" she asks.

I push my short fingernails into my palm just to try to get a taste of the sting she felt. I shake my head. "I guess. Go on."

"Okay. Pretend you're Mom. You can't interrupt."

"I can't believe you'd do that."

"You can't speak! Be quiet or you won't hear the rest."

Scottie talks about the blood, the needles jutting from her hand, how she climbed back onto the rock pier like a crab with a missing claw. Before she returned to shore, Scottie describes how she looked out across the ocean and watched the swimmers do laps around the catamarans. She says that the ones with white swimming caps looked like runaway buoys.

Of course, she didn't see any of this. Pain makes you focused. She probably ran right to the club's medic. She's making up the details, making a better story for her mother. My eldest daughter had to do the same thing—

knock herself out to get some attention from Joanie. Or perhaps to take the attention away from Joanie. Now Scottie is realizing what needs to be done. I'm afraid it's all going to start again.

"Because of Dad's boring ocean lectures I knew these weren't needles in my hand but more like sharp bones—calcitic plates, which vinegar would help dissolve."

I smile. Good girl, I think.

"Dad, this isn't boring, is it?"

"Boring is not the word I'd use."

"Okay. You're Mom again. So I thought of going to the club's first aid."

"Good girl."

"Shh," she says. "But instead, I went to the cute boy and asked him to pee on my hand."

"Excuse me?"

"Yes, Mom. That's exactly what I said to him. *Excuse me*, I said. I told him I hurt myself. He said, *Uh-oh. You okay?* Like I was an eight-year-old. He didn't understand, so I placed my hand on the counter. He said a bunch of swear words then told me to go to the hospital or something. *Or are you a member of that club?* he asked. He told me he'd take me there, which was really nice of him. He went out through the back of his stand and I went around to meet him. I told him what he needed to do and he blinked a thousand times and used curse words in all sorts of combinations. He wondered if you were supposed to suck the poison after you pulled out the needles, and if I was going to go into seizures. He told me he wasn't trained for this, and that there was no way he'd do that to my hand, but I told him what you always tell Dad when you want him to do something he doesn't want to do. I said, *Stop being a pussy*, and it did the trick. He told me not to look and he asked me to say something or whistle."

"Scottie," I say. "Tell me you've made this up."

"I'm almost done," she whines. "So I talked about the records you had beaten in your boat. And that you were a model, but you weren't all prissy, and that every guy at the club was in love with you but you only love Dad because he's easy like the easy chair he sits on all the time."

"Scottie. I have to use the bathroom." I feel sick.

"Okay," she says. "Wasn't that a hilarious story? Was it too long?"

"Yes and no. I have to go to the bathroom. Tell your mom what you told me. Go talk to her." She can't hear you anyway, I think. I hope.

Joanie *would* think that story was hilarious. This bothers me. The story bothers me. Scottie shouldn't have to create these dramas. Scottie shouldn't have to be pissed on. She's reminding me of her sister, someone I don't ever want her to become. Alex. Seventeen. She's like a special effect. It wows you. It alarms you, but then it gets tiresome and you forget about it. I need to call Alex and update her. She's at boarding school on another island, not too far but far enough. The last time I called, I asked her what was wrong and she said, "The price of cocaine." I laughed, asked, "Seriously, what else?" "Is there anything else?" she said.

She's very well known over at Hawaii's Board of Tourism. At fifteen, she did calendars and work for Isle Cards, whose captions said things like, *Life's a Damn Hot Beach.* One-pieces became string bikinis. String bikinis became thongs and then just shells and granules of sand strategically placed on her body. The rest of her antics are so outrageous and absurd, it's too boring to think about. In her struggle to be unique, she has become common: the rebellious, privileged teen. Car chase, explosion, gone and forgotten.

Despite everything, her childishness, her utter wrongness, she makes me feel so guilty. Guilty because I catch myself believing that if Joanie were to die, we'd make it. We'd flourish. We'd trust and love each other. She could come home. We used to love each other so much. I don't call her even though I need to tell her to fly down tomorrow. I can't bear to hear any accidental pitch of joy or release that may slink into her voice or my own.

Scottie is sitting on the bed. Joanie looks like Sleeping Beauty.

"Did you tell her?" I ask.

"I'm going to work on it some more," Scottie says. "Because if Mom thinks it's funny, what will she do?

What if the laugh circulates around in her lungs or in her brain somewhere since it can't come out? What if it kills her?"

"It doesn't work that way," although I have no idea how it works.

"Yes, but I just thought I'd make it more tragic, that way she'll feel the need to come back."

"It shouldn't be this complicated, Scottie." I sit on the bed and put my ear to where Joanie's heart is. I bury my face in her gown. This is the most intimate I've been with her in a long time. My wife, the speedboat record holder. My wife, the motorcyclist, the model, the long-distance paddler, the triathlete. "What drives you, Joanie?" I say into her chest. I realize I've copied one of her hobbies and wonder what drives me as well. I don't even like motorcycles. I hate the sound they make.

"I miss Mom's sneezes," Scottie says.

I laugh. I shake with laughter. I laugh so hard it's soundless and this makes Scottie laugh. Whenever Joanie sneezes, she farts. She can't help it. A nurse comes in and opens the curtain. She smiles at us. "You two," she says. She urges us to go outside and enjoy the rest of the day.

Scottie agrees. She looks at her wristwatch and immediately settles down. "Crap, Dad. We need to go. I need a new story."

Because the nurse is still in the room, I say, "Watch your language."

. . .

At the beach club, the shrubs are covered with surf-boards. There has been a south swell, but the waves are blown out from the strong wind. I follow Scottie into the dining room. She tells me that she can't leave until something either amusing or tragic happens to her. I tell her that I'm skipping paddling practice and am not letting her out of my sight. This infuriates her. I tell her I'll stay out of her way. I tell her to pretend I'm not there.

"Fine, then sit over there." She points to the tables on the perimeter of the dining room. There are a few ladies playing cards at one of these tables. I like these ladies. They're around eighty years old and they wear tennis skirts even though I can't imagine they still play tennis. I wish Joanie liked to play cards and sit around.

Scottie heads to the bar. The bartender, Jerry, nods at me. I watch Scottie climb onto a barstool and Jerry makes her a virgin daiquiri, then lets her try out a few of his own concoctions. "The guava one is divine," I hear her say, "but the lime makes me feverish."

I'm pretending to read the paper that I borrowed from one of the ladies. I've moved to a table that's a little closer to the bar so I can listen and watch.

"How's your mom?" Jerry asks.

"Still sleeping." Scottie twists atop her barstool. Her legs don't reach the metal footrest so she crosses them on the seat and balances.

"Well, you tell her I say hi. You tell her we're all waiting for her."

I watch Scottie as she considers this. She stares at her lap. "I don't talk to her," she says to Jerry, though she doesn't look at him.

Jerry sprays a swirl of whipped cream into her drink. She takes a gulp of her daiquiri then rubs her head. She does it again. She spins around on the barstool. And then she begins to speak in a manner that troubles me. She is yelling as if there's some sort of din in the room that she needs to overcome.

"Everybody loves me, but my husband hates me, guess I'll have to eat the worm. Give me a shot of Cuervo Gold, Jerry, baby."

Jerry cleans the bottles of liquor, trying to make noise.

I wonder how often Joanie said this. If it's her standard way of asking for tequila. It makes me wonder how we managed to spend so much time at this place and never see each other at all.

"Give me two of everything," Scottie yells, caught in her fantasy. I want to relieve Jerry of his obvious discomfort, but then I see Troy walking toward the bar. Big, magnanimous, golden Troy. I quickly hide behind my newspaper. My daughter is suddenly silent. Troy has killed her buzz. I'm sure he hesitated when he saw her, but it's too late to turn around.

"Hey, Scottie," I hear him say. "Look at you."

"Look at you," she says, and her voice sounds strange. Almost unrecognizable. "You look awake," she says.

"Uh, thanks, Scottie."

Uh, thanks, Scottie. Troy is so slow. His great-grand-father invented the shopping cart and this has left little for Troy to do except sleep with lots of women and put my wife in a coma. Of course, it's not his fault, but he wasn't hurt. He was the driver and Joanie was the throttle-man because Troy insisted he wanted to drive this time. Rounding a mile marker, their boat launched off a wave, spun out, and Joanie was ejected. When Troy came in from the race alone he kept saying, "Lots of chop and holes. Lots of chop and holes."

"Have you visited her?" Scottie asks.

"Yes, I have, Scottie. Your dad was there."

"What did you say to her?"

"I told her the boat was in good shape. I said it was ready for her."

What a Neanderthal.

"Her hand moved, Scottie. I really think she heard me. I really think she's going to be okay."

Troy isn't wearing a shirt. The man has muscles I didn't even know existed. I wonder if Joanie has slept with him. Of course she has. His eyes are the color of swimming pools. I'm about to lower the paper so he'll stop talking to Scottie, until I hear her say, "The body has natural reactions. When you cut off a chicken's head, its body runs around, but it's still a dead chicken."

I hear either Troy or Jerry coughing.

"Don't give up, Scottie," Jerry says.

Golden Troy is saying something about life and

lemons and bootstraps. He is probably placing one of his massive tan paws on Scottie's shoulder.

I see Scottie leaving the dining room. I follow her. She runs to the low beach wall and I catch her before she jumps off of it. Tears are brewing in her eyes. She looks up to keep them from falling, but they fall anyway.

"I didn't mean to say dead chicken," she cries.

"Let's go home," I say.

"Why is everyone so into sports here? You and Mom and Troy think you're so cool. Everyone here does. Why don't you join a book club? Why can't Mom just relax at home?"

I hold her and she lets me. I try to think if I have any friends in a book club. I realize I don't know anyone, man or woman, who isn't a member of this club. I don't know a man who doesn't surf, kayak, or paddleboard. I don't know a woman who doesn't jog, sail, or canoe-paddle, although Joanie is the only woman I know racing bikes and boats.

"I don't want Mom to die," Scottie says.

"Of course you don't." I push her away from me and bend down to look in her freckled brown eyes. "Of course."

"I don't want her to die like this," Scottie says. "Racing or competing or doing something marvelous. I've heard her say, 'I'm going out with a bang.' Well, I hope she goes out choking on a kernel of corn or slipping on a piece of toilet paper."

"Christ, Scottie. How old are you? Where do you get

this shit? Let's go home," I say. "You don't mean any of this. You need to rest." I imagine my wife peaceful on her bed. I wonder what she was thinking as she flew off the boat. If she knew it was over. I wonder how long it took Troy to notice she wasn't there beside him. Scottie's face is puffy. Her hair is greasy. It needs to be washed. She has this look of disgust on her face. It's a very adult look.

"Your mother thinks you're so great," I say. "She thinks you're the prettiest, smartest, silliest girl in town."

"She thinks I'm a coward."

"No, she doesn't. Why would she think that?"

"I didn't want to go on the boat with her and she said I was a scaredy-cat like you."

"She was just joking. She thinks you're the bravest girl in town. She told me it scared her how brave you were."

"Really?"

"Damn straight." It's a lie. Joanie often said that we're raising two little scaredy-cats, but of all the lies I tell, this one is necessary. I don't want Scottie to hate her mother as Alexandra does. It will consume her and age her. It will make her fear the world. It will make her too shy and too nervous to ever say exactly what she means.

"I'm going swimming," Scottie says.

"No," I say. "We've had enough."

"Dad, please." She pulls me down by my neck and

whispers, "I don't want people to see that I've been cry-ing. Just let me get in the water."

"Fine. I'll be here." She strips off her clothes and throws them at me, then jumps off the wall to the beach below and charges toward the water. She dives in and breaks the surface after what seems like a minute. She dives. She splashes. She plays. I sit on the coral wall and watch her and the other kids with their mothers and nannies. To my left is a small reef. I can see black ur-chins settled in the fractures. I still can't believe Scottie did such a thing.

The outside dining terrace is filling up with people and their pink and red and white icy drinks. An old man is walking out of the ocean with a one-man canoe held over his head, a tired yet elated smile quivering on his face as if he's just returned from some kind of battle in the deep sea.

The torches are being lit on the terrace and on the rock pier. The soaring sun has turned into a wavy blob above the horizon. It's almost green flash time. Not quite yet, but soon. When the sun disappears behind the horizon, sometimes there's a green flash of light that sparkles seemingly out of the sea. It's a communal activ-ity around here, waiting for this green flash, hoping to catch it.

Children are coming out of the water.

I hear a woman's voice drifting off the ocean. It's far away yet loud. "Get in here, little girl. They're every-where."

Scottie is the only child still swimming. I jump off the wall. "Scottie!" I yell. "Scottie, get in here right now!"

"There are Portuguese manowars out there," a woman says to me. "The swell must have pushed them in. Is she yours?" She points to Scottie, who is swimming in from the catamarans.

"Yes," I say.

My daughter comes in to shore. She's holding a tiny man-of-war—the clot of its body and the clear blue bubble on her hand, its dark blue string tail wrapped around her wrist.

"What have you done? Why are you doing this?" I take the man-of-war off of her with a stick; pop its bubble so that it won't hurt anybody. My daughter's arm is marked with a red line. I tell her to rinse her arm off with seawater. She says it's not just her arm that's hurt—she was swimming among a mass of them.

"Why would you stay out there, Scottie? How could you tolerate that?" I've been stung by them hundreds of times; it's not so bad, but kids are supposed to cry when they get stung. It's something you can always count on.

"I thought it would be funny to say I was attacked by a herd of minor wars."

"It's not minor war. You know that, don't you?" When she was little I would point out sea creatures to her but I'd give them the wrong names. I called them minor wars because they were like tiny soldiers with impressive weapons—the gaseous bubble, the whiplike tail, the toxic tentacles, advancing in swarms. I called a blowfish a blow-pop; an urchin, an ocean porcupine; and sea turtles were saltwater hard hats. I thought it was funny, but now I'm worried that she doesn't know the truth about things.

"Of course I know," Scottie says. "They're manowars, but it's our joke. Mom will like it."

"It's not manowar either. It's man-of-war. Portuguese man-of-war. That's the proper name."

"Oh," she says. She's beginning to scratch herself. More lines are forming on her chest and legs. I tell her I'm not happy and that we need to get home and put some ointments and ice on the stings. "Vinegar will make it worse, so if you thought giraffe boy could pee on you, you're out of luck."

She agrees as if she were prepared for this—the punishment, the medication, the swelling, the pain that hurts her now and the pain that will hurt her later. But she's happy to deal with my disapproval. She's gotten her story, and she's beginning to see how much easier physical pain is to tolerate. I'm unhappy that she's learning this. She's ten years old.

We walk up the sandy slope toward the dining terrace. I see Troy sitting at a table with some people I know. I look at Scottie to see if she sees him and she is giving him the middle finger. The people on the terrace gasp, but I realize it's because of the sunset and the green flash. We missed it. The flash flashed. The sun is gone. The sky is pink and violent looking. I reach to grab the offending hand, but instead I correct her gesture.

"Here, Scottie. Don't let that finger stand by itself like that. Bring up the other fingers just a little bit. There you go."

Troy stares at us and smiles a bit. He's completely confused.

"All right, that's enough," I say, suddenly feeling sorry for Troy. He may really love Joanie. There is that chance. I place my hand on Scottie's back to guide her away. She flinches and I remove my hand, remembering that she's hurt all over.

We are at the hospital again even though it's late at night. Scottie insisted on coming. She practically had a tantrum.

"I'll forget the exact sensations that I need to communicate to Mom!" she screamed.

She still hasn't showered. I wanted the salt water to stay on her. It's good for the wounds. She cried on the way over here, cried and scratched at herself. Her stings are now raised red lesions. A nurse gave them attention. She gave her some antibiotics as well. Scottie has a runny nose; she's dizzy and nauseous though she won't admit it's from swimming with poisonous invertebrates. She's miserable, but I have a feeling she won't do anything like this again. The nurse shaved her legs to get rid of any remaining nematocyst. Now Scottie is admiring her smooth, woman legs.

"I'm going to start doing this all the time," she says. "It will be such a hassle."

"No, you're not," I say. I say it loudly and it surprises both of us. "You're not ready." She smiles, uncomfortable with my authority. So this is what it's like.

We're going to stay the night. I'm sitting on the end of the bed putting eye drops in my eyes. We don't even look like visitors. We look like patients: defeated, exhausted from the world outside. We have come in for shelter and care and a little rest. The staff here has been so kind and lenient toward us. It's nine o'clock in the ICU. We have walked in unannounced; Scottie has received free medical attention. This can't be standard practice. It's over. I know their indulgence of us is because they have no hope, or they've been advised by Dr. Johnston to scratch hope off of their charts. People become so kind right before someone dies.

Scottie opens the curtain and lets the night in—the dark palm trees and the lights of other buildings. She asks me if she hurt the urchin as much as it hurt her. She asks me why everyone else calls them manowars. I tell her I don't know, in reply to the first question. I don't know how that works. For the second question I answer, "Words get abbreviated and we forget the origins of things."

"Or fathers lie," she says, "about the real names."

"That, too."

She climbs up on the bed and we look at Joanie in the half-moon light. She leans back against my chest. Her forehead is beneath my chin. I move my head around. I nuzzle her. I don't talk about what we need to talk about.

"Why is it called a jellyfish?" Scottie asks. "It's not a fish and it's not jelly."

I say that a man-of-war isn't a jellyfish. I don't answer the question, but I tell her that she asks good questions. "You're getting too smart for me, Scottie."

I can feel her smiling. Even Joanie seems to be smiling, slightly. I feel happy, though I'm not supposed to be, I guess. But the room feels good. It feels peaceful.

"Water," I say. "And blankets." I leave the room to get water and blankets.

When I come back to the room, I hear Scottie say, "I have a remarkable eye." I stop in the doorway. Scottie is talking to her mother. I watch.

She is curled into her mother's side and has maneuvered Joanie's arm so that it's around her. "It's on the ceiling," I hear her say. "The most beautiful nest. It's very golden and soft-looking and warm, of course."

I see it, too, except it isn't a nest. It's a browning banana, the remnant of our old game still stuck to the ceiling.

Scottie props herself onto an elbow, then leans in and kisses her mother on the lips, checks her face, then kisses her again. She does this over and over; this exquisite version of mouth-to-mouth, each kiss expectant, almost medicinal.

I let her go on with this fantasy, this belief in magical endings, this belief that love can bring someone to life. I let her try. For a long time, I watch her effort. I root for her, even, but after a while I know that it's time. I need to step in. I tap lightly on the door. I don't want to startle her too badly.

Final Girl

Emma watches her son and thinks, This is it. It's all over now. He is looking at himself in the square mirror that hangs on a whitewashed wall over his bathroom sink. She's a bit disgusted with him, but knows that this is unreasonable. Keoni smiles, jaw clenched, and leans toward his reflection, ponders his teeth. He tries to pat down his longish, wild hair. It isn't coarse but it's wavy and fluffy, soaring above his forehead. Keoni talks to his hair. "Just back down," he says. "I won't hurt you."

She has an excuse for entering his bathroom—she places a bowl of gardenias on the countertop—though she doesn't have a reason for staying. She invents a few. She fingers the counter for dust. She walks behind him and opens the wooden jalousies. Outside, the Indian coral tree's branches creak and snap. The leaves on the mock orange hedge flutter against the panes, shedding scent into the room; twig shadows move across the red tile. She bends down and smells the sleek petals of the gardenias. The rich spicy smell contends with bitter orange and the dusty earth scent of stems. She plucks a black ant from a petal's coil and presses it between her fingers.

"I haven't done the laundry in your room," she says. "Bring everything out for me, okay?" She wonders if he'll think it strange that she hasn't gotten it for herself as she always does, but he doesn't think it strange, she can tell, and this makes sense to her, his failure to notice subtleties.

"Okay," he says. "But we should go. Kids will be coming."

Emma looks at her watch. Young trick-or-treaters would be arriving soon.

Keoni tries out angles with his head, flexing his jaw, sizing himself up. She wants to feel comfortable with him. She wants everything to be, to feel, the same. She decides to join him in the mirror, says, "Move over, hunk," then stands beside him and makes pensive, pouty faces until he barks out a burp that forces her out of the room by its sheer volume and eggy smell. She tells him she'll be waiting in the car. She walks down the thin corridor and covers her mouth with her hand, bites on the band of a ring, then bites on the jewel, an orange turquoise. Now, because of recent findings, her aside, her calling him hunk, seems inappropriate. Whoops, she thinks. Oh God.

From the car, Emma looks at her plantation home, the grassy expanse it rests on, the hedges that enclose it. Her family has occupied this home since 1837 and Emma finds it sad that her ancestors could not know its future residents or see that it's been kept in the family through the years, through hurricanes and divorce, death and disease. The house looks windswept even after its restoration. It's a tough house, proud of its resilience to weather, to sun and salt, welcoming it even, with open sliding glass doors as if it thrives on storm. Keoni would live here with a wife and children. Whom would he marry? She watches him walk out of the house. She watches the way he moves. She thinks his style is thoughtful and artless at the same time. Every item on him references some other era or place or culture. His hat makes him look like a newspaper boy from the fifties. His unbuttoned shirt is a silk vintage aloha shirt, pre—Pearl Harbor, the design uncluttered and bold. His baggy pants are a trend she believes has lasted far too long. She watches the cuffs of his pants sweep the sand on the walkway. Where does he get this? This cocky gait. Emma is aghast. This child. This creature. This living boy. He slumps slowly toward the car. He winks at her and she feels an urge to smack him. Who taught you that? she wants to yell. He winks like Ben, whom Keoni has never even met, and winks aren't genetic, are they? You can't inherit a wink. She wonders where Ben is. She has always assumed he returned to Moorea, but she cannot know for sure. She imagines him standing in the ocean he claimed was bluer than toothpaste, winking. She wishes she could just borrow him for a day. She needs a father for her son, but one that can be used then returned after services are rendered.

Earlier today, Emma cleaned the living room, the laundry room, the gutters, the sea-glass windows, discovering lost possessions behind the washer/dryer and atop the summits of cabinets. She gathered things that needed to be laundered—clothes, slipcovers, towels, sheets—and this chore led Emma to the cluttered universe of Keoni's room, busy with the tokens of his many passions—surfboards, motocross posters, helmets, an assortment of shoes and video games—Aggravated Burglary, Assault and Battery II, Demon's Lair, Rippin' with Tony Hawk; it led her to his bed, a sleigh bed, which always made Emma feel cozy at night when she thought of Keoni asleep in his sleigh, snug in the plaid bedding he insisted on having once he outgrew He-Man and Spider Man, heroes he now deems to be totally gay.

She began at the bottom of the bed, loosened the nurse's corners of the top sheet, the tuck of the bottom sheet, and of course it caught her eye—the slickness of it, the way it seemed to glow. She stared at it, knew immediately what kind of magazine it was. She did not open it. She did not touch it. There was a girl holding pom-poms on the cover and Emma thought of high school, of not making the cheerleading squad. She remembered Alika Chai, a football player, the reason she wanted to be a cheerleader. She was in love with Alika Chai until rumor had him climbing up to Mrs. Churchill's roof, masturbating, then ejaculating down her chimney. Emma was so confused and sickened, and then tremendously relieved that her kicks hadn't been high enough, her splits not close enough to the ground.

Keoni was so young. Just thirteen. Is this normal? she wondered, and a disappointment came over her, a fear, because she realized just how normal it was. She saw his new tennis shoes and picked one up, as if it were evidence of goodness and normalcy: a shoe, but then that shoe made her think of grade school, when the children were allowed to go barefoot, though she never did. Pepper Well was her only friend. She was also from a plantation family. Pepper Well had a carnival-huge teddy bear and she'd get naked and hump this bear, reenacting for Emma the things she'd seen her father do to the woman who owned a gallery of dolphin art and on the side sold huli huli chicken. Her dad caught Pepper humping the bear. He kicked Hubby across the room then made Pepper get dressed and face the wall for twenty minutes.

Emma remade Keoni's bed. If she caught him smoking she'd show him pictures of blackened lungs, but there was no punishment for this. She couldn't take him to a gynecologist and have him look at a real, unairbrushed vagina. Before leaving his room, she made sure there was no evidence of her ever having been there.

They drive along the beach road. Keoni waves at a friend, Sunny Russ, a boy with a cadaverous chest who is always flipping his hair and patting his bare stomach. Emma waves at Sunny and smiles. She pretends it was his room. She attaches the entire act to him, a boy with a father who can slap him on his back, give him a sip of his beer, and tell him it's time he start doing his own laundry. She watches Sunny in the rearview mirror. He takes out a cape from his backpack, fastens it around his neck.

"What's he supposed to be?" Emma asks.

Keoni turns to see his friend. "Gay," he says.

"Come on," she says. "You've always dressed up."

"I can't think of anything to be. This one girl thinks I should be a pirate—like Captain Cook or something."

"Who is this 'one girl'?" Emma asks. "Anyone special?"

"I don't know," Keoni says, smiling into his fist. "She's cool, I guess. She's really political." He turns up the stereo. He sings and slaps the air with his hands. He nods his head to the music's deep throb and Emma thinks he looks like a car toy you affix to the dash. They are going to buy candy, but she feels this isn't enough.

Perhaps she needs a costume—she could be a witch, or a bat, a batty witch. Tonight is the night of the souls, the night of the ghosts. She isn't ready to take on the monsters. She wishes it were Easter instead. Bunnies and chickies—this she could do.

Keoni reaches over and honks the horn at a pale man standing in the middle of the road videotaping a street sign: NAWILIWILI ROAD. "Move, haole," he says.

Emma shakes her head. Lately, he's been using the word a lot, a word that literally means "foreigner," but inside the case of the word is the implication of whiteness, dumbness, invasion. It always amazes her when he says it. Under his dark tan and light rum skin is her skin—the color of cashews, almost the same coloring as the man standing in the road.

Her childhood was nothing like Keoni's. She gave him a Hawaiian name. He had Polynesian blood. It was that easy. She envies this, his easy existence. He doesn't seem to be affected by his father's absence, or by race, class, anything. If he was a girl, Emma thinks, he'd be dressed in black and curled in bed reading tragedies. She has always, selfishly, wished he were more unfilled, more destitute, had just a bit more of that character-developing sadness. Instead he's a child who sings in the car. Instead he's content with life, with her, free to socialize at beach bonfires and beach clubs alike. Her parents and their circle of friends made it impossible for Emma to slip under the radar of the local gaze. Her parents' parties were infamous. Their lethargy legendary.

They played and lounged like colonists. After a ninth-grade history lesson, kids at Emma's small school took to calling her Ms. Manifest Destiny. Her father's side of the family descended from missionaries, so her name was on school buildings, churches, and hospitals. *Here comes the missionary. Assume the position.* This was what the kids by the stream would say when she'd try to join their bonfires. If anyone bothered to get to know her, they'd find that her family wasn't even religious, much to Emma's dismay. She yearned for a kind of family her ancestors had—one in which children wore bonnets and mothers read stories that had subliminal warnings and moral directions—but her family didn't even say grace, just, *Thank the Lord for Lilacs!* Lilac was the cook.

"This is taking forever," Keoni says. "I want some candy. Gotta get me some sugar." He honks her horn again.

"Please don't do that," Emma says. "It draws attention."

Tourists are strung along the main road trying to find things to take pictures of or searching for things to buy. Emma doesn't begrudge them this. She understands the need for proof. Sometimes, guiltily, she feels that Keoni is her proof. By having him, she is somehow more authentic, more deserving of the land she lives on.

There are a few celebrities about because a film is being shot at the hotel, so this keeps the herd even more alert. She can see the hotel from here, perched on a cliff, pink in the sun, overlooking the bay. She cannot help but think of Keoni's father when she sees this hotel—it was even grander then, more formal, and Ben looked so hopeless and untidy next to its marble pillars. She once loved him for this. When he left without saying good-bye, she'd go to the bay and bury her pregnant self in the sand; letting the tide rise, feeling the sand tighten and press around her. She felt as if she were being swal-lowed. As time passed, she scoffed at things she once liked about him. He came from Moorea to determine the effects of low-frequency sound on marine animals. What an uninteresting question, she thought. She forced herself to only remember the small quirks about him that bothered her—his frayed shorts, his fishy smell, his loathing of people who studied dolphins, and that his favorite color was infrared. For almost a year she was led to believe that he was the only horrible charac-ter in play when really there were two more.

Emma looks at her hand on the steering wheel, the ring her father gave her in the hospital after giving birth. The jewel looks like a sunset and she knows now that this was a monetary transaction. Be content, he was saying, and I'll give you sunsets. I'll give you a home.

Her father evenutally told her what really happened, admitting it was his idea to send Ben away, his obliga-tion as a major shareholder of R. Estate Partners, which owned seventy-five percent of Kauai's land. They couldn't have someone from a foreign place inheriting Kauai, her father said. She immediately saw the hypocrisy of his statement. *Inheriting Kauai*, Emma said aloud. She imagined the island being plucked from the Pacific and dropped into her lap.

Her father spoke more on the topic of acquisitions and threats, as if finally realizing she was the only beneficiary. One threat was a landowner who blamed the decline of her people on Western explorers, merchants, and missionaries. She wanted the assets and income derived from R. Estates to support schools for Hawaiians only. Since Ben was of indigenous pedigree, as her father put it, he had a heart that was likely to bleed. "Do you get me?" her father asked. Emma did not, or at least did not want to. He spoke of more specific problems to better illuminate her. "They want us to make those Hanalei lots accessible. More beach access, land access, hiking trails. Don't you see the problem with this? The public won't stay within those access corridors; they'll wander onto the adjoining land—you get me? They'll snoop, steal, vandalize, plant marijuana, and relieve themselves whenever they want to go to the bathroom. He took the money, Emmy. You remember that."

Emma comes to a complete stop and waits her turn behind a line of cars to cross the one-lane bridge. She looks over at Keoni, at his hat worn backward, his melted slouch, his fingers dancing to the thump of one of his CDs. She notices that the top of his lip looks strange, bigger than normal—it seems swollen. She reaches to turn down the stereo to have a better look. Keoni faces her and says, "Mom! I'm listening to that." She sees then that it's a pimple, a blemish, how awful, distorting his mouth like that. Did it just spring up in the car? She looks ahead, drives until they are forced to stop again. She feels Keoni's eyes on her.

"What?" she asks.

"Nothing," he says.

She realizes he's looking past her, his eyes grazing over something beyond her. She sees a woman in a yellow translucent pareu, bending over to pick up a hair clip. The late sunlight passes through her skirt, revealing the curve of her thighs.

"She dropped something," Emma blurts.

"Yup," Keoni says. "Lost a barrette."

How observant, Emma thinks. Really. "Really," she says.

"Really what?" he yells over the music.

"Just really."

He looks at her, confused, and then: "Really Nilly, a fly girl from Philly, forget La di Da di she's a new school party. It's cold, so chilly, that must be my ice queen sporting rock-a-billy like some heartland ho. . . ."

Emma cannot respond.

At Foodland she says, "Let's split up. I need a few normal groceries. You get the candy."

Keoni gives a little laugh. "Roger that." He lobs on his backpack.

Emma watches as he struts down an aisle. She calls after him, "Grocery hopping!" because when he was little, that's what he thought it was called and would hop down the aisles. He doesn't look back at her, but at the end of the aisle he grants her one small hop. Emma wonders if he'll be bigger when he returns because he seems to be getting bigger by the hour. When he walks into her bedroom, her Limoges collection always shakes on the shelves. She secretly wanted him to stay a small boy, lithe and compact, but things aren't working out that way. She wonders if his magazine is still there, cozy under his covers, tucked in. She goes to the magazine aisle. The one she saw in his room has a different cover now. A girl dressed as Catwoman is centered on the cover looking sexy and annoyed. Two girls stand behind her—a sexy Dorothy and a sexy Snow White—and both seem astonished by their endowments; their mouths make tiny o's. Ben was the only person she knew who bought this regularly. It surprised her at the time. She thought that only lonely, homely people read it, or Eastern Europeans longing for America. She thinks it such an odd, annoying coincidence that Ben read this magazine, then realizes the coincidence is not so extraordinary, but rather something most fathers and sons have in common whether they know it or not. She touches the glossy cover. The sulk of a painted mouth. A stiff, angry boob. She feels alone. This is something she will never fully understand; something, another thing, that Keoni and Ben have in common, a realm she can't enter—their skin, their sex. Both exclude her. She considers stealing the magazine and placing it alongside the books on the coffee table—books she cherishes, more for their history than their contents. They're books that belonged to the first mission family—hymnbooks, music books, a family Bible, and a quarto Bible with apocrypha. Also on the table is a book of her ancestors' correspondence from 1836 to 1872. Would Keoni see how ridiculous his magazine was if placed next to this history? Would he understand the message? She imagines her son skimming through the shiny pages of girls with panties hooked to one side. She imagines him with his penis in hand, once referred to as pee pee, then, later, willy, and then one day it became something that was his entirely, not to be addressed by her. The grocery lights are bright. They make her feel yellow, infected.

Keoni sits in the living room waiting for kids to come to the door. Emma puts away groceries. She always told Keoni that his father was a good man, soft-spoken, sensitive, serene. The idea was to protect him, and somewhere within her she believed her rendering to be true. So focused on the transaction designed by her parents, over the years she ignored the fact that Ben took the money and left without speaking to her. Now she is remembering burying herself in the sand and the ache of abandonment and betrayal. She is remembering the exact amount of money it took for him to leave, and she's thinking of the boy in the other room, his boy, and how she never considered that one day he'd be bigger than her. She wonders if her portrayal of Ben has been a mistake. If Keoni thinks too highly of him, if he believes that his truer, better roots are elsewhere.

Emma hears the doorbell ring. She hears it ring for the second, third, fourth time. She enters the living room. Keoni is crouched below the window, eyes above the sill, peeking.

"What is this?"

"Shhh!" he says. He motions for her to get down, and Emma shakes her head and makes her way to the door then stops and thinks, Why not? She gets down on her knees and crawls to the window.

Outside are two toddlers with mustaches painted on their faces. They wear ties and shiny black shoes. The man they're with, their father presumably, has a pacifier in his mouth and is wearing an adult diaper over his jeans.

"That's the most disturbing thing I have ever seen," Emma says.

Keoni crawls toward the calabash bowl he has left on the table in front of the couch. He brings it back and the two of them pick at its contents as the threesome outside gives up and walks away. If only life were like this and you could pick what you want, she thinks, and just throw out the rest. She'd pick her mother's hands. She'd pick her father's charm, his ability to make life's complexities anecdotal. But this game is endless. And there'd be a cost to any sweet she chose to take or throw away. It's basic economics. Textbook lessons. Like the Mongoose Solution, a remedy the government once employed—importing mongooses onto the islands to kill the snakes and rodents. They killed the snakes, but they killed the chickens, the eggs, and the indigenous birds as well. There is always an exchange, an unforeseen penalty. She imagines a mongoose, the sparkly slit of its eye, its ravenous hunger. She imagines it swallowing a warm, defenseless egg.

"Look," Keoni says. "Here's more."

They duck down. "What are they?" Emma asks.

"No clue. Oh wait, they're characters from that cartoon. With the dogs that look like rats, or rats that look like dogs. I forget. College kids like it. They *relate*."

Emma looks at her son, or the boy who resembles him. "They're so cute," she says. The tallest of the bunch picks up the littlest to let him ring the bell. "Oh, we have to answer. We really should."

"No," Keoni says. "Let's just watch. It's fun like this. Next year we'll open the door."

"It's not that fun," Emma says, but it is. They have a perfect view of these children's faces, their anticipation of the door opening, their hopeful belief. The children eventually walk away. On to the next door. The night proceeds in this manner: Children come. Trick or treat. Children leave, disappointed. Emma feels cruel and oddly happy. A breeze sifts through the house, sucking the cream and rust-orange silk curtains through the window. She can see the gusty beach from here, the sand waltzing, the glint of the dark, moody water. The waves boom like bombs.

"What do we have here?" Emma says, as three girls approach the door and ring the bell.

"Trick or treat," one says.

"Lick my teat," another says.

"Let's open the door," Keoni says.

Emma frowns. She bites her ring. Her legs are sore. Falling asleep. She crouches lower and her blouse dips down, revealing her breasts, her white, pinching bra. She doesn't readjust. She looks at them. She compares them to the furious boulderlike breasts of Catwoman. She peeks out the window. Who are these girls supposed to be? Are they even in costumes? One is dressed in a white collared shirt and jeans; practically identical to the outfit Emma wears. Another wears a skirt and blazer and has some sort of badge pinned to her shirt. The third girl has Farrah Fawcett–style feathered hair, a halter top, and skimpy Dove shorts.

"What in the world?" Emma crouches down lower. There is nothing more frightening to her than teenage girls. They roam in packs like wolves. The girls are perhaps sixteen, confident in their costumes; they ring the bell and knock on the door with their fists and their shoes—penny loafers, black pumps, and tan sandals. The girl in the white shirt pounds her fists on the door and screams, *Help! Somebody!* The girl with feathered hair screams as if she's being tortured, while the girl with the badge knocks persistently and says with a tough southern accent, "You need to open this door. You need to open this door right now."

"Holy shit," Keoni says.

"What are they doing?" Emma doesn't want to get caught peering at them. "I don't like this."

"Mom, they're not serious. They're only acting." He looks at the girls, entertained, fascinated, but Emma isn't looking anymore. She sits down and faces the other way, afraid. Afraid of what? Young girls laughing. Young girls making her door shake.

"Let's just open it," Keoni says. "They're obviously dying for some candy."

"Don't you dare," Emma says, grabbing his sleeve. "They're on drugs. Something is wrong with them."

"God, Mom, you sound like such a dork."

"Respect the rules of this house, please."

"Is one of the rules don't answer to trick-or-treaters?"

"This was your idea. Be consistent."

"But they're screaming."

"Don't let those girls in, Keoni," she says, but he dismisses her with a "Just relax already."

"I said no," and now she doesn't even care if they come in or not. She just wants him to listen to her, to obey and understand her. She wants him to be like her. He stands up, not listening, and she feels as if something between them is coming to an end.

"Mom. Seriously." He picks up the bowl.

As he reaches to open the door she says, "You're going to meet your father. I'm sending you to meet him."

It's too late for him to respond. Now he has three girls to contend with. Three girls who fall into the house, screaming, "Trick or treat! Took you long enough."

Keoni's usual cool disappears. He has the big boy curse. He looks old, but he's just a boy.

He offers the bowl of candy, eyes downcast. Emma is standing now, eyeing the girls.

"Nice house," one of them says.

"Thank you," she and Keoni say at the same time.

"It's, like, austere-chic," one says.

"Like Hester Prynne meets Charo."

"You girls aren't from here," Emma says.

"No. L.A. We're here with Laurie's dad." The girl in the suit points to the girl who looks like a normal girl, who says, "He's working on a movie. He's a professional arguer. My name isn't really Laurie—it's my character's name."

Keoni puts the bowl down on a side table. "Help yourself," he says, then walks to the couch and opens one of his magazines.

Emma watches the girls sift through the bowl of Gobstoppers, Milk Duds, Blow Pops, and Sugar Babies, candy, Emma believes, that are the most difficult to eat.

She tries to catch Keoni's eye, to see the results of her directive, *you're going to meet your father*, the cost of it. His eyes are glazed over. He lowers his head, reaches up, and twirls a lock of hair around a finger.

"What are you supposed to be?" Emma asks.

The girls look up. Two have lollipops stuck in their mouths. The girl Laurie serves as their spokeswoman. She says, "Final Girls. The girls in horror films who don't get killed." She goes on to tell her what movies they're from and Emma nods with recognition.

The girl with Dove shorts pipes in, proud of their idea. "They were the ones who beat the monsters and outlasted everyone."

Emma can picture so clearly who these girls are without their disguises. Practically the same girls. A kind of girl Emma never got to be. "Clever," she says.

"Always," one says, and they all laugh.

One girl looks at Keoni. "Hey, right on for finally letting us in."

"Sure," he says from the couch.

"This is my son, Keoni," Emma says. "He wanted to let you in. He thought you were cute." He glares at her. She has found her punishment.

The girls walk toward him. "What are *you* supposed to be?" they ask.

"Nothing."

"Why don't you come out with us, Mr. Nothing? Come trick-or-treating."

"Sure, honey," Emma says. "Why don't you go out with them? Three girls. Real ones."

"No thanks," he says, still glaring at her.

"He raps," Emma says. "Show them."

"Shut up," Keoni says.

"You're good, honey. Sing what you were doing for me in the car."

"I wasn't singing for you. I was just messing around."

"Do you like West Coast or East Coast?" a girl asks.

"East," he mumbles.

"I do, too," Laurie says. She drops a few Sugar Babies on the floor then looks up at the ceiling and says, "Rest in Peace, Biggie. R.I.P. B.I.G."

The other girls roll their eyes.

Emma has no idea what anybody is talking about.

"Well, we'll be around your neighborhood if you want to catch up."

The trio shakes Emma's hand as if they had been houseguests. The girl with the skimpy outfit says, "I was promiscuous but I still survived."

Emma realizes she is referring to her character and not herself.

Laurie says, "I was the first girl to kill a monster, or at least I thought I did. Sequels."

The last girl says with an accent, "I was the first female in a horror film to be victim, pursuer, and hero. And I had a good relationship with my monster."

And then they leave, roam on to the next house. For a second, Emma considers running after them, catching up.

"Oh my God, Mom," Keoni yells as soon as the door closes. "What was that? Why were you trying to embarrass me like that?"

"I wasn't. I thought you'd jump at the opportunity to be with those girls. You like girls, obviously."

"What are you talking about?"

"I'm talking about girls."

"Is this about that lady today? I was just looking at her. I didn't mean to—she was just right there!"

Emma likes how panicked he is. "Well, you sure enjoy looking at them. Maybe you should talk to them."

"I do talk to them; there's a girl I talk to all the time, but you were there pushing me. You made me feel like a kid with special needs or something. I don't understand what you're doing."

"I don't understand what you're doing."

"What do you mean? Why are you mad at me? Why are you sending me to meet my dad? Where are you sending me anyway? I don't get it."

She can tell that he's yelling to overcome the quaver in his voice. "I'm not mad at you." She goes to him, sits beside him on the couch. She should tell him he's not going anywhere, that she was angry and confused, that she made it up, but she wasn't confused.

"It's cool, though," Keoni says. "I want to meet him. I want to know that part of me, you know?"

He is looking at *Road and Track*, avoiding her eyes.

"Oh," she says. "I see." She needs to face the consequences of her lie. "Are you sure?"

"Yeah," he says. "Yeah, I'm sure."

"Well then, this is exciting," she says, deciding to let it go on a little longer. Just a minute longer. She will time it. She watches her son imagining Ben, hoping for Ben, picturing his looks, their possible similarities. From this brief amount of time, he will understand anticipation and loss, eagerness and devastation. He will understand how life can be stolen. It will bring them closer together. It will return him to her.

"What do you mean by part of you?" she asks. "What part of you do you need to know about?"

"Just, you know. I don't know. His side of me."

"The better side, you mean?"

Keoni looks at her warily. "I thought you said you don't know where he is."

Emma puts her hand on Keoni's neck; she massages and kneads his muscles. She brings his head down to her lap and strums her fingers through his hair. He relaxes under her hand.

"When did you speak to him?" he asks.

She doesn't answer. She thinks of the three girls, imagines herself with them. She could be Carrie— Final Girl and monster, right? And victim. She asks Keoni to hand her the book of letters from the table in front of them, letters written mostly in this house. They ignore the doorbell. He tugs on his hair then passes her the book of correspondence.

"'Dear Brethren,'" she reads. "'It is my duty to serve as missionary teacher among the heathen. We are doing well as to health, however of the 6 bundles of bibles only 2 have been delivered. Also, Capt. A does not behave himself so well. He threatens that if the native women are restrained from visiting the ship he will seize our taro and pigs.'"

"Why are you reading that?" Keoni asks. "It's so lame."

"It's where we come from," she says. "It's important. It's just as important."

"I don't like it," he says. "Let's talk about my dad. What happened? When am I going?"

" 'Natives are almost always coming in for food and have taken a liking to our musketoe netting and camphor trunks,' " she reads.

"Stop reading that," he says. "I already know about that stupid stuff. Where does my dad live? Tell me about him. Tell me what happened."

The vines of trees swing and whine. She catches glimpses of the backyard when the curtains billow; she sees the wraparound porch, the monstera that surrounds it. "You want to talk about your dad? That part of you?"

"Yes," he says.

"Well, you're right," she says. "I have no idea where he is. He left us. I begged him to stay with me, to start a family here, to make it work, and he deserted us after my family had given him so much love. Your grandparents did everything they could to keep him here, offered him things, even. I don't know why I said I was sending you to meet him. I made a mistake. He was not a good man." She wonders if this is how her parents felt when they lied to her. It feels strange to hate them yet understand them so well. She understands their longing for permanence, their desire to write their own history.

"What's wrong with you?" Keoni yells.

Emma closes the book. A breeze brings in the tart rot of white guava. Keoni's head rises off her lap and she feels a coolness there, then a coldness. He wipes his eyes forcefully the way men do when they cry—slap away their tears. He looks around, she thinks for something to throw. He rips some pages out of the book of letters, balls them up, and throws the old-smelling paper at her cheek, then walks out the front door.

Emma continues to stare at the backyard, notices the monstera is pocked with bites. It must be because she finally obliterated the weeds, the insects' usual fare, under the gardenia bush. She wonders when Keoni will return. She hopes he returns having learned to take pride in the right things. Their name is on churches and school buildings. She waits for him. She sits and waits.

The doorbell rings. She walks to the window and looks out without ducking down and hiding. Keoni stands before the door, his hair windblown, his back lengthened out of its habitual slouch. He looks wounded yet strong. He sees her in the window, and she feels so sorry for him—his rebellion was so short. He had nowhere to go, nothing to do. But then she sees someone else on her porch. A girl sitting on a settee. A girl in a triangle bikini top and a grass skirt. "Trick or treat." Keoni opens the door and walks into the house holding the girl's hand.

"This is my friend," he says. "Kayla. She's in my class."

Friend? Emma holds on to the doorknob and tries to feign indifference, but knows she isn't succeeding. Keoni looks smug. She remembers that men don't wallow, they act; she sees that Keoni is a man.

"Hello," Emma says. "Nice to meet you, Kayla."

After the Final Girls and everything else that has happened tonight, this girl seems convenient, store-bought, an escort hired for revenge, yet she remembers him mentioning something about a girl—a girl he talks to. The political girl. She is beautiful, her skin rich and polished. She makes Emma feel old. She sees faint, golden hairs on the girl's dark arms. The color of the hair matches the dried leaves of her skirt. "So, I guess you're a hula dancer?" Emma looks at Keoni, who is looking at Kayla's stomach, then face, then long black hair.

"She's a heathen," he says, and the girl laughs and looks down at her bare feet. He gives her arm a tug and they begin to walk hand in hand toward his bedroom. The girl waves at Emma—she has chipped orange polish on her short nails.

"Where are you going?" Emma asks.

"My room," he says.

"And why are you going there?" Emma laughs and crosses her arms over her chest. "What are you going to do?"

"We're going to find me a costume."

Their arms swing as they walk. They try to trip each other. They laugh.

"I'm going to go out after all." He stops walking, but the girl continues down the hall without him. She'll help him find a costume, an identity, but for one night only. He turns to face Emma. "That was mean what you did," he says. "But I'm sorry that happened to you. To us."

Emma has tricked him. He believes her story and why wouldn't he? She wonders how long this has been going on in this house, these family tricks, these family games, these cunning transactions. I'll give you sunsets, she thinks. I'll give you a home.

"What are you going to be?" she asks.

He shrugs his shoulders.

"Be careful," she says. "Check your candy. People can be nasty."

"I know," he says, and he walks to his room, to his girl, perhaps believing that he gets to decide who he'll get to be.

House of Thieves

We are floating on our surfboards in a loose circle beyond the break so we can talk about the emergency: Wendy's brother is back. "What does he want?" Nicole asks. She's holding the nose of Wendy's board to keep from drifting away.

"I don't know," Wendy says. "Maybe he wants to come home."

Belle is tucking her breasts back into her bathing suit top. They are getting really sloppy. I look down at my chest. I have nothing to fix and arrange. I'm twelve.

"Did he look good?" Belle says.

"I guess," Wendy says. "I didn't see him up close."

Wendy is sad, though I could be wrong. I'm a writer and a diarist and also an actress at the Diamond Head Theatre so sometimes I see things that aren't really there. We are moving farther away from shore, past the rocky fingers of reef. The water here is a blackish blue. I'm thinking about Wendy's brother, but also about sharks. Echo Point is known for having them. We're all gripping our surfboards between our thighs. The sun stings our backs; eight legs dangle in the water. To any sharks below us, we must look like sea turtles. When I tell this to the others, they lie on their stomachs. Sometimes my prose is very effective.

"He was swimming at our beach," Wendy says. "He must have used the access by the lighthouse."

"Whack-job," Nicole says.

Wendy shrugs her burning shoulders. "It's his beach, too, I guess."

"Why don't we like him?" Belle asks.

"I like him," Wendy says. "He just makes me angry sometimes."

"I like him," I say, even though I feel guilty about it. I know that her brother has done more than steal a car. Belle and Nicole think Perry's just a runaway thief who has abandoned Wendy and scarred her emotionally. My dad scarred my mother emotionally. He has a license plate that says SUE EM. My mom divorced him then sued him, but now they're back together again. They dance on our balcony to "Shake Your Groove Thing," their second wedding song.

"He's a thief, that's why we don't like him," Nicole says. "He's come to take our money, I bet, but we'll kick his ass. We'll egg him."

I imagine how we'll do it, like the Sharks and the Jets. I choreograph fight sequences: Pas de bourrée, kick kick, neck hold. Pirouette, layout, punch punch, jazz hands. If we get caught for fighting or vandalism I will simply say that we're just kids growing up on an island, doing bad things in pretty places. I test this line on my friends because it sounds stylish and dramatic and just right.

"Niner," Nicole says, which is this week's term for loser.

Sometimes my verse doesn't work so well, but Nicole's a skank and I take this into consideration. She's always reaching behind her legs to pull the flesh of her inner thighs apart and saying, "If I looked like this I'd be perfect." Tomorrow, at Secrets, or Old Man's, or No Place, I will drop in on all her waves. I'll do a cutback. I'll pump my board and ride out a wave to shore like a boy. This is how I win arguments with Nicole, my third-best friend.

We paddle in closer to shore. There are no waves. We're lifted and dropped by swells that don't break or take us anywhere. "Let's go," Belle says. "This sucks."

"You go," Nicole says. "You suck."

Belle and Nicole are sisters. They don't like each other much, in a sisterly way. On dry land they wear their dad's scrubs—just the pants part. They pair them with bandeau bikini tops and claim that the other has copied.

"Race you," Nicole says. She splashes water on all of

us and it's freezing since we've been cooking in the sun. Then she paddles in so fast her arms blur like insect wings. Nicole gets babysat by this white pill her parents force her to take, and it makes her either freak out, or focus intensely on inanimate objects, or get angry and cranky and two-year-old-like. I've caught her sucking her thumb.

Wendy doesn't want to go in, I can tell. Seeing her brother again has upset her. It's truly a disaster. He's really sweet and really real and handsome, but he moved out of the house when he was sixteen because he accidentally touched her inappropriately or something. I know this because I accidentally caught a glimpse of her Dec. 12 entry in her old diary. The glimpse said something about them playing Escape from Sing Sing. She was eight years old. He'd give her five seconds to escape from his room before he tackled and pummeled her. One time he tackled her and they starting kissing and their mom found them kissing and touching inappropriately. She called a professional who was like a referee but with a pen and weird glasses. The family hugged and cried. Wendy is a good writer. Due to the suspense she created I couldn't help but read more. The entries stopped on Feb. 18 with this very emotional paragraph: *When he said he was sorry I thought he meant for the charley horse, but maybe it's cause of the before part. Now he's going to the North Shore. He stole Dad's car, but Dad's not telling. I'm worried for Perry.*

Because he banished himself, I find myself truly believing that Perry's a good person, noble even, like the Christ figures in the plays I've been in. I got to play a Christ figure once. I played Annie in *Annie*. In addition to being noble, Perry is a very good long-term connection for us because we're planning to live in Haleiwa one day on the North Shore. It's where all the real surfers live—Mark Occhilupo, a.k.a. Occy, a.k.a. the best surfer ever, Shaun Tomson, Curren, Hans, the Ho brothers, and the lost-at-sea legend, Eddie Aikau. I know their stats and bios, their likes and dislikes, their favorite bands, their sponsors, if they have a cat or a dog or a wife. Perry is just like these guys. He used to be the best of the amateurs. We watch his old contest videos, which proves Wendy has forgiven him for whatever happened. When he surfs he looks like he's doing something illegal. I bet one day he'll have his own line of shoes.

Wendy stays by my side as we paddle in though she can go much faster. She's the strongest girl I know. I feel so lucky that we like to surf even when no one's looking. I feel lucky that we aren't girls who sunbathe, although I know that Belle and Wendy have given blow jobs. Nicole told me what a blow job was and I can't see why a guy gets pleasure from someone blowing on his dick. My friends are in seventh and eighth grade and they have knowledge I don't have yet. I can't wait 'till November when I'll be a teenager. I can date guys like Perry and it won't be considered harmful to my childhood. Except now he's twenty-one—I think that's still in the danger zone. I want to be older. I hate my grade.

Kids my age listen to Tiffany and Debbie Gibson and know nothing about Oingo Boingo or life.

When we aren't surfing or hitchhiking or sliding down Maunawili moss slides into pits of mud so we look like the boys in that movie *Lord of the Flies*, we hold car washes to raise money for summer concerts and for Budweiser, but if any customer asks, the money is for children with some sort of disease. We have the wash at Wendy's because she has a circular driveway right off the avenue. Her house looks exotic and Greek and breakable. It slopes toward the ocean. It flickers at night. It has an alarm that sounds like the sirens in last month's production, *The Sound of Music*. I played one of the von Trapp children. All the other child actors were Hawaiian and Filipino. I had artistic problems with that, but our director said, "You try finding actors in Hawaii who aren't Hawaiian or Filipino." Onstage, next to my brothers and sisters, I looked like dandruff.

No one's coming to our car wash. Nicole stands on the side of the street trying to lure them in. She's wearing boxers, a men's V-neck Hanes with holes in both of the armpits. She takes off her shirt, showing off her black bathing suit with buttons down the sides. She rolls the waist of her boxers down—it's how we all wear our boxers and trunks.

"What if Perry comes to the wash?" Nicole asks.

"Someone will come," Belle says, "if you keep standing there looking like a Waikiki hooker. You're going to get us all raped."

"You do look like an asshole," Wendy says.

Nicole smiles; she takes to teasing well. She believes it's something the less fortunate do for survival. Her goal is to be a surfer-slash-model, which totally hurts our cause.

I remember the customer who asked us if we gave body washes. He was old, maybe thirty. It was weird because all of us got really shy. We're usually loud and wise, but when he asked us if we would wash his body, we just giggled and said no. We never giggle. Nicole still hasn't learned that we can't act how we're used to acting because those actions make perverts horny and that's why we wear baggy clothes.

I'm sitting on the low rock wall, letting the water from the hose run over my legs. Wendy is helping a worm right itself. I like her so much during the day. At night, I miss her. I realize she has older girl things to attend to, like drinking without making a scene and blowing on dicks, but I'm always left with evil Nicole. Sometimes Nicole and I drink and play Jem and the Holograms, but whenever I talk about it the next day, she just stares at me in a disgusted way.

"Nicole, 'member my killer solo last night?" I ask her this for everyone to hear.

"I remember that you suck," she says. Her voice echoes off the cliffs so I hear "you suck" three times.

"Do you really want Perry to come home?" I ask Wendy. I want to tell her that I know her secret and she shouldn't be ashamed. It was like playing dress-up or physical therapist. We've all done it. We've French-kissed our stuffed animals and even each other sometimes. It's pretend. It's practice.

"Of course I want him home," she says. "We're best friends."

This hurts my feelings. "If you're best friends then why doesn't he ever come to see you? Why'd he abandon you?"

"He hates our parents. It has nothing to do with me."

Nicole comes in from the street, takes the hose from me, and holds it above her head, lets the water run down her brown, burned hair and small body. There are bumps on her skin from the cold. She puts her mouth to the stream of water and drinks. I wish I looked like her. She reaches around and grabs the insides of her thighs and looks down at the triangle of space between them. "If I looked like this, I'd rule," she says, then turns to me. "So, Kora, what are you going to do?"

Steel Pulse is playing at the Shell tonight and everyone's on my case for not chipping in. Wendy's having the car wash at her house and her neighbor is buying the beer; Belle and Nicole stole their mother's canned goods and returned them to the grocery store for cash.

"Better ask your parents to give us a ride," Belle says. "Kora Kora."

No way. Around my parents, I belt out show tunes and perform plays that I've written or updated or regionalized. If they knew that I drank beer, even though I fake my drunkenness most of the time, they'd think I had been putting on an act the entire time, impersonating an innocent girl. I try to get us off the topic, and then on the avenue I see a car slowing down, blinker blinking. The plants surrounding the driveway are quivering wildly, warning me. It's called foreshadowing, when things quiver, like my "Maybe" solo in *Annie*, my lonesome trembling voice foreshadowing that maybe my parents would pick me up, but maybe not. I should have known he'd come.

"Hide our money," Nicole says.

"We don't have any, stoops," Belle says.

Perry drives in slowly. The stolen car has black surf racks on its roof, Billabong and Straight Up stickers on its side windows. The car seems happier this way, filthy with reddish dirt. We part ways for it. I stare at him, his messy hair and sad face, the scars between his eyes and on his chin. I have to admit I've dreamt about him one or five times. I haven't seen him since he came to our school last year and gave Wendy a brown bag full of mangoes.

He is banned from their house. Wendy says it's because her parents think he's unstable and that he lives like a wild animal with an arrow in its ass. I feel sorry for him. I imagine his life with boys and hard alcohol. It's so Mohican. His eyes are murky. I'm looking right at them and have no idea if they're seeing me or not.

"Fill her up," he says. His voice is scratchy and nice. We get to work because we don't know what else to do.

We play it cool. We head to the rear of the car, bend down so he can't see us in any of the mirrors, and we mouth questions at one another. I keep an eye on Wendy. She hoses his car and I rub it with the chamois. Nicole brushes his rims with a toothbrush, then stops and scratches her face with it. Belle polishes the hood ornament—a silver woman with wings. We're all watching Wendy work her way up to the front of the car with her hose.

"Hey," he says, and she looks up. We all look up.

"Let me see you," he says. Wendy is washing his door now; before she can do anything his hand is cupping her chin, turning her head from side to side and then to face him again. "Uncanny. You look like my sister."

Wendy smiles but it comes out lumpy and twisted because he's still squeezing her face. "Okay," she says, "let go," and like that, he does. He turns up the volume on his stereo and laughs.

"Are you okay, Perry?" Wendy asks.

"I'm fantastic," he says.

The music is so loud I feel as if I'm at a festival. We dance as we wash his car. Nicole rolls across the hood. There goes her kicking-his-ass plan. I stand on the roof and scrub his racks. We wash the car with extra soap because it's so dirty. We move around it as if it's a bonfire. Perry turns on his wipers. He swings his hands together and apart, conducting a symphony of girls.

Wendy stands in front of the car's windshield, aims the hose at Perry, and shoots. Perry lets his tongue hang out of his mouth, pretending he's dead.

When Wendy's done rinsing, we dry the car. We wipe the cloudiness off his chrome bumpers until we see blown-up, ugly versions of ourselves.

"Five bucks," Wendy says.

Perry laughs. He doesn't look at her. He doesn't seem to look at anything. I wonder if he's sleepwalking. "Spot me?" he says to the steering wheel.

"Fine," Wendy says. "Family discount. You better go, I think. For now."

"How's the parentals?" he asks. "The old peas."

"They won't like that you're here."

"So? What do they like?"

"They liked this car. You've ruined it."

"I've translated it," he says, and I believe we could be soul mates.

"I'm going to get in trouble," Wendy says. "You're allowed to come back. They just want you to do it properly, with your act cleaned. Mom will go into shock if she finds you hanging around here."

"She's already in shock," he says. "Her face is stapled that way. And you're not getting in trouble. Have we ever been in trouble? Come on."

"They say you're on drugs."

"I'm not right now."

"Are you drunk?"

"Not yet."

"We're hungover," I say.

Wendy's glare at me is harsher than the sun's. "It's been a year," she says. "You just show up, then disappear."

"Are they here?" he asks.

"No. Golf benefit thing."

"When will they be here?" he asks, looking at the rock wall surrounding his home.

"I don't know," she says.

"They just leave you by yourself, don't they?"

"Sometimes. I tell them Katrina is watching me—my Surf Club coach." We all laugh. It's a brilliant scheme. We tell our parents we're going to Surf Club because *We're going to Surf Club* sounds better than *We're going to hitchhike around the island looking for surf and stuff to egg.* They believe Katrina exists because Wendy's parents hire people to do everything. We joke that she probably has a lightbulb-screwer-inner. She used to have a running coach, a fat Serbian man who wore sweat suits and smoked cigarettes and yelled, "Pump the arms, girl! They are the tickets to the run!"

"What assholes," Perry says. "They're unbelievable. Parents should come with warning labels. Mom's could say, 'Warning: I may cause dizziness and loose stools.'"

I wish he had a diary that I could accidentally read.

"Why was your car so dirty?" Nicole asks. "It looked like a pterodactyl took a huge diarrhea on it."

"Gross," Belle says. "That is so gross."

"Shut up," Nicole says. "It's nature."

Perry laughs, or appears to be laughing. It's a slow, bored, gagging sound. "The hills," he says. "I take it off-roading. You guys should come with me one day. Good fun. One day." He gets out of the car and peers over the

wall so he can see his home. He wears his shorts low
on his hips, and I can see his V-shaped muscle and a trail
of dark hair going from his belly button to down below
his drawstring. There's sand stuck to his back, and the
splotches make formations. I feel as if I'm gazing at the
sky, finding objects in the clouds.

I imagine us going off-roading with him, rolling off a
cliff then landing upright in the ocean. We bob toward
the real America, the middle of it, where girls are hefty
and corn-colored and I have a chance of being not ugly.
I say, "Now, this is a road trip," and everyone grins and
nods like experienced hippies. Perry could make our
lives sensational.

"You should come home," Wendy says. "I'm not
mad."

"It's not that. It's not because of that stuff. I mean,
when you start seeing how superficial things are you'll
see that it's better . . . to not be . . . that. Fuckin' golfing,
man. Back then, we were just kidding around. It's cool,
right?"

Only I know what they're talking about, kind of. I'm
not sure what happened really. It seems Wendy isn't sure
either. It hurts me that she has never talked to me about
it. I tell her everything.

Wendy is looking down at her toes and nodding her
head. "It's cool," she says. "Did you come here to talk to
Mom and Dad?" She begins to sniffle and Perry hugs
her for a long time. They're best friends again and now
I'll have nobody. He wipes her face with his thumbs.

"Are you coming home, then?" Wendy asks.

"Sure," he says. She hugs him again, but his arms have dropped to his sides. "Soon," he says. "Actually, I came by to get some of my stuff. Some clothes, some jewelry, some of my art. Can I come in real quick? Then we'll cruise somewhere. I'll take you cliff-jumping or something."

No one says anything.

"I really need my things," he says.

Wendy shrugs. "I don't know. I think you should wait. We could hang out now, and then come back."

"Nah, let's do this together before they come home." He smiles and pokes her in the ribs. "When I move back, it will all be here again. Like it never happened."

"Well, if it's your stuff," Wendy says. "We can move it back together, too."

"This shouldn't take long if you guys help me." He says this to the rest of us. "Everything in the pool cottage is mine, so if you want to load that up, I'll see what I've left in the house."

The plants are foreshadowing all over the place. Wendy punches in the code.

We load his things into the trunk: the stained glass with the pretty pink roses, the silver and the china, the glass chandelier. In the pool cottage, a warm room full of old-smelling things, Wendy hands us objects, explaining what they are just as her mother does. She shows us something called a French Quimper urn and a hot milk pot. She looks sad handing me a framed map of the United States she says her father loves, but I tell her it's outdated, pointing to all the mistakes. Belle and Nicole fight the entire time over who gets to carry what and the best way to pack a trunk. I wonder if Wendy really believes he's going to bring it all back.

We place two capes of red and yellow feathers over the heap in the trunk. They're beautiful. Hundreds of small feathers. Wendy tells us that they once belonged to a king and queen. She says they're priceless but I think they're worth a lot. I think of Wendy's parents— her dad with his skinny legs, her mom with her freckled hands—and it makes me feel bad.

"I like stealing," Nicole says. "Maybe he'll take us surfing now."

Perry meets us at the car with a laundry basket full of liquor, shoes, watches, and jewelry. He tells us to move some small things from the trunk into the backseat to make room for the basket and something else of his that he needs to get. He takes five more trips back into the house, coming out each time with pieces of white marble.

"What's all that?" Belle whispers to Wendy.

"My fireplace," Wendy says.

Perry tells us thanks for the hands. His car is white and shimmering. The radiator grille reflects the sun into our eyes.

"What about cliff-jumping?" Wendy asks.

"Or surfing," Belle says.

"I'll come back tomorrow."

"You promised," Wendy says.

"No, I didn't."

Wendy looks like she's going to cry and I can't bear it. She obviously still needs me to be her best friend. "Wait," I say. "Give us a ride to the Shell tonight."

His eyes dart to me—it's like he's noticing me for the first time. I stand up straighter. "You owe us," I say.

"Fine," he says. "Come unload this stuff with me, then I'll bring you back to your little concert. You can see how the other half lives."

Belle and Nicole are excited, looking forward to being seen with him in the slow-moving traffic through Haleiwa. We have access now, and they can't bother me for not chipping in. Wendy doesn't look so happy. She stays outside while the three of us get in the backseat. We elbow one another as we see all of the silver on the floor—the carving knives, the ladles, and something Wendy called a pickle fork. The backseat is filled with small, pretty things that mothers love. We're criminals now, and that seems original.

When I see Christopher step out from the mock orange hedges I'm sort of relieved. Christopher Fallafasafau, Wendy's landscaper guy, is a magical man, always suddenly appearing from the bush. He has a voice like a woman's and he wears Samoan skirts. I feel safe when he's around. He's very close to nature. Sometimes, we call him Christopher Fall Off the Sofa and he smiles very adoringly at us when we do this.

I want to get caught and sent home. I want to be with my parents. I'm scared now, and it makes me angry that I can't stick to the one, tougher feeling. I'm scared because this is my idea and Belle and Nicole don't know everything. I could be wrong about Perry. What if he isn't noble? What if he's like Stanley Kowalski? Christopher will save us. Samoans are the salt of the earth.

Perry stops arranging the trunk. He takes a drink from a bottle that has red wax dripping down its sides. "Is there a problem?" Perry asks Christopher, which is very ballsy considering Christopher looks like a linebacker even in a skirt.

Christopher looks at all of us and says, "Nope." He turns on the hose and waters his plants. "Think I could have that when you're done?" he says to Perry.

Perry puts the cap back on the bottle and hands it to him. "Here you go," he says. "Mahalo." He winks at Christopher.

This makes me feel incredibly lonely. Wendy gets in the front seat, looks back at me, and scowls. Perry digs another bottle out of the trunk and gets in the car. We pull onto the avenue and drive away from our neighborhood.

Belle says to Nicole that this will be so fun, that we'll feel like royalty when we get out of the car at the concert. I imagine wading through the public toward the thump of the Shell. Nicole says that we'll look like royalty, but from some really messed-up kingdom, like the Thunderdome. She points to Perry. He's head-banging to the music and when he hits his head on the steering wheel he blames his parents for it. I buckle my seat belt.

Driving into Haleiwa sort of wins me over and relaxes me. This place is the cool capital of the world. In third grade Hawaiiana I learned that *hale* means "house" and *'iwa* means "handsome person" or "thief." An 'iwa is also a bird that steals food by forcing other birds to throw up. We are finally in the place we'll call home one day: the House of Thieves, the House of Handsome People. The House of Barf-Eating Birds.

Even Wendy has her head out of the window. Every car has a surf rack on it, and every boy has baggy shorts and ratty hair. They nod at Perry when he drives by. The air smells like salt and hamburgers.

We cross over the famous bridge and head to his house. It's not as nice where he lives. The places we passed on the way were cute because they tried to look like beach shacks, but the houses in his neighborhood really are beach shacks. When we get there, late in the afternoon, we unload some things from the backseat. The air is colder now. The ocean is becoming dark and choppy. This is when the sharks swim closer to shore to eat their suppers.

Perry tells us to drop what we have in the living room.

There are two guys sitting on the couch, hunched over the coffee table looking at a poster of sumo wrestlers. The guys are very dirty. I think they're twins. Nicole smiles at them but they don't look at her.

"Why would you want a picture of two fat mother-fuckers rolling around with each other?" one of them asks.

"Shut up, tweaker, these guys are the heroes of their country."

Perry throws two watches at them. "Now leave me alone," he says. "My sister's here."

The guys look up and see the four of us and start to laugh. "Dude has family," one says.

Perry tells us to leave the rest of the stuff in the car and to wait here while he showers. The house is very messy. The carpet is sticky. "This place is disgusting," Wendy says. "Why would he choose this?"

We have nothing to do but listen to these guys argue, so we do that. I wait for a turn to jump in the conversation.

"They get a lot of respect, a lot of money, beautiful wives."

"So what, dick? They're fat. If those guys cruised over here, all anyone one would say is, 'Hey, look at those two fat guys.'"

"They make more money than skinny guys, you fuckin' 'tard."

Nicole laughs. The guys both look at her. One of them imitates her laugh. I have never seen Nicole embarrassed. I thought I'd like it but I don't. She picks up a magazine from the floor and pretends to read it. We all pretend to read it. We all pretend to belong here. Wendy doesn't look at the magazine. She glares at the boys.

"Still," one says. "Who'd want to make money being a fat guy throwing another fat guy out of a ring? How do they get so fat?"

"Two things. Beer and pasta."

"Are you pros?" I ask. "We're going to live out here and be pros one day."

The boys begin to laugh hysterically. One turns to the other and, with a high voice that doesn't sound like mine at all, says, "Are you a pro? Can I lick your pro balls?"

Wendy takes the magazine from Nicole's hands and throws it at them. "You guys have ruined my brother. You've ruined him!" This makes them laugh harder and throw things at each other and say "rad" over and over again. We follow Wendy on her search for Perry and find him in a back bedroom smoking a cigarette. He's naked, wet, and standing in front of a window. He looks skinny and sickly. His butt is bright red. He looks like a liar.

"Sorry," he says, covering himself with a sheet. "I don't use towels. I haven't used a towel in three years." On a plastic crate—the only furniture in the room besides a mattress—are a few beers and a bottle of pills with Wendy's mother's name on it.

"Please give us a ride home," Wendy says. "You come back, too. You shouldn't stay here."

"I'm never going back to that shit hole," he says.

"You said you were. You promised."

"Stop it with that Boy Scout promise shit," he says. "Listen, I can't drive. Sorry, Sis. I've got tons of change, though." He won't look at her. "Sorry to disappoint. Sorry you're growing up, but believe me you're not stuck here. You're stuck there."

"What are you talking about? I'm stuck here. You promised you'd take us back. Take us home!"

I can't look at Wendy. Her voice is like the voice I hear in my head when I read her diary entries—young and afraid. I can't look at Perry either.

"Look, it's for your own safety," Perry says. "I shouldn't drive when I'm this messed up. I showered but it didn't work. Look, I'll see you kids later. Don't do drugs. Don't play golf."

"Fuck you, Mr. T," Nicole says.

He laughs and smokes and spits into a bottle of beer, then sways in place.

"All I wanted was to hang out with you," Wendy says. "I thought you wanted to hang out with me again." Perry turns back to the window. Belle puts her arms around Wendy and tries to lead her out of the room but Wendy bends over and begins sifting through a pile of his clothes and crying. "I remember this shirt. I always wanted to borrow this shirt. I always tried to dress like you."

"Take the shirt, Wendy. Jesus."

"Screw you," she says, and her voice changes into something I don't recognize. She punches him in the arm and he sweeps out his leg to trip her. It's the quickest tripping maneuver I've ever seen.

"Escape from Sing Sing," he says.

"Let's go," Nicole says.

"Yeah, come on," Belle says.

Neither of them understands what Perry has just said. I take Wendy's hand, pull her up, and push her toward the door. "Escape," I say, looking her in the eye, hoping she knows I know. "Five seconds." Something in her expression changes. It's as if she's agreeing with me, thanking me.

I expect her to leave but instead she shoves Perry onto the bed; what's left of his beer spills onto his chest and he laughs and dabs at himself with the sheet loosely wrapped around his waist. She grabs the bottle and hands it to me then punches her brother in the face. He reaches to grab her, suddenly sober. I throw the bottle at his head as hard as I can and he just looks at me, stunned. Beads of blood form near his eyebrow. It's a strange color, his blood, similar to raw ahi tuna. Our stares puzzle him and he touches his eyebrow then looks at his hand.

"Little bitch," he says.

Nicole, not wanting to be excluded from anything, punches him in the stomach as he tries to get up, and Belle pulls off his sheet. We stop and stare. I close my mouth, but it falls open again and then suddenly we are all laughing at the sad slug between his legs. I retrieve the bottle because Perry looks ready to strike, but then he turns on his side, away from us, and curls his body into a hook.

"Go," Wendy says, and we run out the door and through the living room. The twins are still arguing.

Outside the scraggly screen door it's dark and the grass is wet; unknown things lurk everywhere. I look at my friends. I have no idea how we'll get home. The wind is so strong.

We stand by the car and watch the front door, but we know he won't come after us. His position on the bed made it seem like he'd never want to get up again. Wendy picks up a rock and aims it at Perry's window. Her arm shakes in the air.

"We've done enough," Belle says.

Wendy drops the rock and I know we won't talk about what happened in that bedroom ever again. Wendy begins to walk toward the big hill that circles the bay. We follow, forming a line behind her because there's a road on our left, a cliff on our right. I'm at the back of the line. There are no streetlights. I can smell sugarcane burning somewhere far away.

"We can walk to a pay phone," Nicole says. "I'll call my dad, even though he's probably delivering a baby."

Dads and babies seem impossible right now. I can't picture either of them. Dads and babies. My mom. My orange cat, Boo. These things make my throat dry.

"I don't want to call Dad," Belle says.

I'm glad she said that because I don't want him, or any of our parents, to see us. Something inside me wants to continue the adventure. I feel scared and cold, but also alive. I look down at the bay and think about the people who will be here tomorrow, surfing the most dangerous breaks. Sometimes I wouldn't mind being swept out to sea and eulogized on T-shirts and bumper stickers. I'd do anything to be considered spectacular. I'd do anything to never be bored, and if we don't continue on this way, we'll become girls. Normal, sunbathing girls.

I hear a car coming. I see a blaze of headlights. Maybe we can still make it to the concert. Belle and Wendy usually do this—flag down a car. They're older, prettier, but I'll see if it's my time yet, if I can get to where I want to go. I see their three bodies in the distance, the stars over their heads. A gust of wind makes their hair fly up and then settle on their backs. I can't tell them apart.

I hold my arm out, stick my thumb up. I can do this.

Island Cowboys

Pete was on vacation, visiting his brother's ranch. This was supposed to be a good thing; he wouldn't have to think about any of his problems. Pete thought of his problems. The company that had prospered in his father's hands was dying in his. His pregnant girlfriend of five years did not believe in marriage. She said she disliked the institution, but Pete had the suspicion that if he were another man, she'd beg for the ceremony. She'd secretly practice the bouquet toss and memorize lines from *The Prophet*. Pete thought of marriage. Of money. He thought of his brother, Kimo, and blushed. Last night, Pete dreamt of sabotaging his brother's ranch, tipping the bulls, kissing his brother's wife; he forgot what else he had done. Pete wondered if he hated his brother. He couldn't decide, and he didn't trust dreams.

As he cooked his eggs he looked out of the large window that framed a square of the ranch, which was hazy and wet this morning. Planks of light came through the wooden fencing. Unseen birds yelled at one another. In the distance, he could see his niece, the dot of her, gathering flowers or veggies. The sight of her made him want to be a teenager again. He could get used to this life. He wished he had chosen it.

The eggs hissed at him. "My eggs are burning," Pete said. "They're burned."

"Stick to the cold stuff," Sophia said. "We should really go to the main house."

Pete didn't want to go to the main house. In addition to his vague, human problems, he had a very tangible animal problem: there was a goat that roamed the dirt road that ran between the main house and their cottage. He wouldn't let them by; he would spit and charge them and look at them funny. Sophia and Pete always wimped out and took the long way over the fence and through the wet pasture, but yesterday Pete decided to go for it, and consequently got reamed. A big dark bruise was taking over the upper part of his hip, moving toward his belly button like an approaching high tide. He wondered if he was more hurt than he thought he was. He could feel a sort of jiggling in his lower abdomen. Pete cupped a hand around his side, pressed his fingers into his gut trying to identify things he didn't know anything about.

"Ready to go?" Sophia asked. "They have pastries at the main house. Oh God. Yes."

Five months ago, Pete knew she was pregnant before she did.

"I've been doing everything to lose weight," Sophia had said. "Dieting, exercising, taking extra Paxil, smoking cigarettes."

"You're pregnant," he had said. "Ha ha! Admit it!"

Sometimes they were stupid like this together. She didn't really smoke cigarettes; she was just reluctant to admit she was pregnant even though the stick said so. They both were skeptical, not wanting to get their hopes up. They had been going at it for two years, trying their best to knock her up. He thought their failure was because she refused to put her legs up over her head, said it was so desperate-looking. He would sigh, imagining all of his good stuff seeping out of her like snot from a runny nose. But at last it worked, although her belly still wasn't that big. The size of the hump in a baseball cap. He loved her stomach, its fleshy verification of lust and love—proof that desire still existed between them. She hardly touched him anymore. Whenever he got an erection, she laughed at it and gave it a quick tug as if it were a funny toy or a sea cucumber.

"Fine," he said. "We'll go to the main house. We'll go the long way. Damn it. I need to tell Kimo to put that goat someplace else. I'm helping him with the bulls. I took care of our parents and the company. It's the least he could do."

"Click," Sophia said. "Your self-pity tank is full."

Pete feared any kind of confrontation with his brother, and relied on self-pitying remarks to make sure his sacrifices were being kept afloat. Kimo's severed relationship with their parents was ample evidence that he had no problem with turning his back and saying goodbye. So long. Pete didn't discuss faults and mistakes with Kimo, not wanting even a dab of bad blood between them, especially now that Pete was verging on becoming a family man himself. He soon would have his own unit, his own operation, and he wanted his child to have a cousin, an aunt, and an uncle. He imagined festive Christmas dinners with their two families, the children silenced by the eerie blue of a lit plum pudding. Also, if the time came, and it was coming, it's what time did, Pete would need his brother to bail him out of financial nastiness.

Pete used a fork to scrape the burned eggs into the rubbish, and then rubbed his hip some. He could use a painkiller about now. Or a scotch, but Sophia would get jealous.

"You should have given that to the goat," Sophia said. "Barter."

"Screw the goat." Pete put the pan into the sink to soak. He forgot that he wasn't supposed to use a fork on the pan. This year, because the guest room in his brother's house was being renovated, they were staying in a cottage that belonged to the ranch hand, who was on the mainland scouting for bulls with good sperm, good estimated breeding values, and a scrotal measurement above thirty-four centimeters. They also had to be handsome, Pete was told. Attractive bulls.

The ranch hand had taped various instructions to various appliances all over the cottage. His pans said, *Do not use metal on me. You will scrape me and I will poison your food and kill you.*

Pete wondered what the ranch hand looked like. He was probably a big burly cowboy with the kind of skin that told stories. The ranch hand was starting in Montana then moving on to Wyoming. Pete would like to go to those places. He imagined that Montana was probably a place where you could walk into a bar with a gun and a big dog, order a beer, and then go out and drive as fast as you wanted to.

Pete watched a cluster of black bulls moping in the sun. A few of them watched him back, but not the biggest of the bunch, the one he liked best. He tapped the window. "Look at me," he said. The big bull walked away and from the side Pete thought he looked like a state on a map. Nebraska. Nebraska headed west. Pete knew nothing about bulls or the actual shape of Nebraska on or off the map.

At the main house, Anne was cooking eggs and sausages and porridge and custard French toast. Anne was perfect. She was a large-animal vet. Papayas and pastries were on the table. Kimo was making fresh orange juice.

"I heard you burned an egg this morning," Anne said.

"Why were you cooking?" Kimo asked. "We've got that taken care of."

"He was seeing what it was like," Sophia said. She was on her third donut.

Pete took a deep breath. "Kimo, I need you to move the goat," he said. "Maybe put him somewhere else. What if that had been Sophia?"

"We think he's going through puberty," Kimo said.

Jane came in and chugged a glass of juice. She was sixteen and always thirsty.

Anne gasped. "Janie. Sweater. Now."

Pete looked at his niece, then quickly looked away. Her cleavage was alarming. She wore a tank top that glittered MEOW across her chest. She caught him looking and shimmied her shoulders, then scratched at the air.

"That's great, Kimo," Pete said, and coughed into a fist. "Could your animals go through puberty on another dirt road?"

"Well," Kimo said, "I don't think I can move him. Just as Morris can't ask me to move out of my house, I can't ask him to move from his road."

"But it's your road. And he's a goat," Pete said. "I mean, Christ, I'm not asking you to slaughter the creature." Sophia, Kimo, Anne, and Jane all stared at him.

"He's a nice animal," his brother said. "Just ask him if you can use his road. That's all you have to do."

Pete didn't believe he was a nice animal—he had a

satanic gummy grin and he clearly had it in for him, but Pete also knew that this conversation was useless—his brother wouldn't move the goat. Kimo had all of these ranch rules and beliefs. A while ago he had learned these new methods for training horses, and now he used these same hypnotic practices on everything, even his bulls, even his cats and dogs. Jane once told Pete that when her dad was angry with her, he'd stare at her, and when Jane left the room, he'd follow her and keep staring.

"Firm and consistent. That's the motto. Soon he's going to start throwing pebbles at me," Jane had said.

That, too, was part of the training system; gently throwing pebbles at the animal.

Pete didn't feel he could question these techniques, or anything his brother did. Kimo was obviously doing something right. "I'm helping you with the bulls today," Pete said, reminding his brother how helpful and accommodating he was.

"Thank you," Kimo said.

Pete considered throwing his glass of juice at Kimo, but supposed that the gesture would be infantile and crazy. He needed a form of retaliation that was collected and shrewd. Pete then thought that his aspiration to think of a collected and shrewd act was, in fact, infantile and crazy.

"Why's his name Morris?" Sophia asked. "That makes him even more creepy."

"It's from a children's story," Jane said. "Don't you

know that?" She sat down at the table next to Sophia, concerned. "About the goat who refuses to bleat or baa, and will only moo and oink? You have to read the story to it." Jane pointed to Sophia's stomach then stared at it for a while, pondering something. "I'll give you my old books, Aunt Sophia. I've got *Ferdinand, The Polar Express,* the Beatrix Potters, *Tikki Tikki Tembo, Blueberries for Sal, Goodnight Moon, Pat the Bunny.* I have them all." Jane reached for a half of papaya. "Jeez, Aunt Sophia, you ate all the donuts."

Sophia smiled proudly then patted Jane on the head and said, "Don't call me Aunt. It sounds so cranky. I don't go around calling you Niece Jane."

"That's true," Jane said. She ate a spoonful of papaya seeds, showed Pete her black, bumpy tongue, then spit the seeds into a bowl.

Kimo spooned the seeds out with his hand and stuffed them into Jane's mouth. "Swallow," he said.

Pete watched her swallow, with difficulty, the bitter seeds he had only seen birds eat.

"You are not a show-off," Kimo said. "You don't do things like that."

When Jane had swallowed the seeds, she opened her mouth wide. Pete could see her tonsils. She took a sip of juice and continued eating her breakfast. Pete was amazed by how calmly she received her humiliation. She reminded him of Kimo when he was young, absorbing their father's cruelty so elegantly.

"How is your stomach so small?" Jane asked Sophia. "You literally ate all the donuts."

"It's in my ass," Sophia said. She got up and turned around and lifted her sweater up over her jeans.

"Good Lord," Jane said. "Baby got back."

Jane began to sing some sort of song. Kimo clued Pete in, calmly explaining that all the songs the kids were listening to these days were about big asses and dollar bills. Sophia danced as Jane sang. Kimo smiled and told Sophia she had a fine rump. Pete did not like this at all. It reminded him that his brother was once familiar with it, was once familiar with all of her. It was something nobody talked about. The conversation would demean everybody. It was the most embarrassing coincidence; embarrassing on a soap-operatic scale. It seemed that so many facets of their relationship were humiliating to Pete. Even their how-did-you-meet story was a story best untold.

Pete remembered the hot day. He had had a flat and had no idea how to change a tire. She had pulled over in an old red convertible and said, "I'm not a lesbian. Everyone I help thinks I am because I know cars, and I'm good with a jack. The conclusion isn't even logical."

He remembered that she had asked if he could hold her hair back because she didn't have a rubber band. He held her hair while she worked on his car, gathering it when it fell, adjusting. The simple act made him feel close to her, necessary, as an intern must feel helping a doctor. And still, after what he assumed was her flirting (she told him she'd had a man behind her pulling her hair before, but never on the side of a highway), he made no move. He had thought that the situation was so pornlike and hated that everything in his life reminded him of a minor version of something ridiculous.

Kimo and Sophia had been young lovers. Kimo: eighteen. Sophia: fifteen. "Kid stuff," she had assured him, and of course Pete wasn't so immature as to be concerned about the past, although he knew that kid stuff could often be much more intimate and lovely. Kid stuff could be the best stuff in a person's life.

Pete watched his brother kiss Anne on the forehead and on the mouth, and then he tipped an imaginary hat. He asked if Pete and Jane were ready.

"Let's go herd the boys," he said.

Pete got on his four-wheeler and rode with Jane behind him, her arms around his waist. Her white fingers clung to his jacket. He felt her cheek on his back. Every now and then she would pull his hair or cover his eyes with her hands and laugh. They headed to the farthest paddock. Their goal was to get all the bulls to the corral by the main house, then wash them so they would look presentable for tomorrow's auction. Even though Pete had been helping his brother with the auction for three years now, he was always amazed as he rode through the acres of pasture, opening and closing the many gates, by what his brother, the former mess-up, had accomplished.

Kimo got kicked out during his senior year of high school for selling goods to the neighborhood junior high—cigarettes, weed, Mad Dog, sunglasses, or whatever he managed to find. Their dad didn't yell at him or ground him. He saw it as an opportunity. He wanted to retire and this way Kimo could learn the import business and take over. In a way, he was already experienced at being a supplier, but Kimo refused. He would never come home and when he did, he would sit on the couch in the living room and throw a tennis ball against the wall. Pete remembered how his dad would just watch him do this until one day he intercepted the ball and pelted it at Kimo's eye and told him it was time to start working for him or it was time to go.

"I want to travel," Kimo had said, and their dad offered to buy him a one-way ticket to anywhere in the world, provided that he earn his own money to make his way back. Kimo picked the Big Island, a thirty-minute trip from Oahu, a twenty-five-dollar fare. Then he picked up and left for good. Pete remembered missing the sound of the ball when he left—its hollow and resonant *boing*.

Pete would relay the ever-changing news about Kimo to his dad, told him he was a hippie in Hilo, or a coffee bean picker in Kealakekua, or that he was in Parker Ranch, helping an older couple with their books and stallions. Kimo never really wanted to hear about their parents—how their father had been expelled from the country club for going from table to table, eating off people's plates. After their dad's stroke there were moments when he couldn't remember Pete's name but could always remember not only Kimo's name, but also the name of his old tennis racket, Hula Girl. Kimo had returned only for their dad's funeral. He'd given a eulogy depicting a family and a father that to Pete were completely unrecognizable.

And now Kimo owned his own ranch with hundreds of Black Angus bulls that sold every year for about seven grand apiece. So many industries were flailing—tourism and sugar, real estate and dot-coms, but not cattle. Not bulls. Pete was in awe, not only by the monetary aspect, but also by how his brother was so self-made. Pete was amazed that there was no punishment for Kimo—no karmic reminder, no turning of fortune's wheel. But yes, it was also the money. Pete had played his cards the way they were supposed to be played—he tended to his mother, protected her from his father, he took over Tower Imports, managed the crew of stevedores. And now the price of paradise was killing him. Last week, while making a payment on his mortgage and his mother's medical bills, he wept. "Why is it so hard to be a citizen?" he had said aloud while sobbing at his desk. It was a moment that pained him to think about.

Pete honked the horn on his four-wheeler. He was determined to have a good time. Jane's grip was hurting his bruised abdomen tremendously, yet he liked it.

"Hold on," he yelled to her. She squeezed him harder and he pretended she was Sophia holding on to him, depending on him. When Jane moved her hands to his arms, he involuntarily flexed. Then he voluntarily flexed.

"Tough," Jane said, pinching his arms. "Aren't you tough."

"Not really," Pete yelled back. He thought of the stevedores who unloaded the docks. They were the biggest men Pete had ever seen. Their biceps looked as if there were beer cans under their skin. Jane made Pete feel like a stevedore. He raced ahead. He loved the air here, so dry and cool. He wished he had a ranch where children could run merrily and be chased by dogs and chickens. His house was on overpopulated Oahu, on Kailua Beach where babies could burn and drown, get stung by jellyfish or eaten by a tiger shark. Undertow, strangers, boat engines whirring like knives—the beach was an ugly place. He didn't feel like living on a beach anymore. He had always lived there. His entire life. His home was suddenly so unappealing—too vacationlike and beachy; in the air the constant drone of summer, that annoying time when everyone jogged and saw bad movies.

Pete raced back to Kimo because he didn't know where he was going. He looked at Mauna Kea, so superior in the high sun, snowcapped and just there—smack in the middle of the island, done with erupting, content. It had played a role in creating all of this. It gave Pete volcanic ambitions: he wanted eruption and upheaval; wanted to alter his familial ecosystem and see what survived.

. . .

When they got the bulls into the auction corral, they took each one aside, locked them in a guillotinelike contraption, and scrubbed them down. The bulls were dirty, especially their backsides, which were caked in crap. Kimo did the faces, Pete did the sides, and Jane got the rears.

"This is bull shit," she said.

Pete thought the bulls liked this hosing down and scrubbing. It must feel good. His side was aching, but it felt as if he had pulled an important muscle. Pete hosed down number 72.

"These bulls have got it made," Jane said. "Tomorrow they'll meet a bunch of cows and they'll just have sex for the rest of their lives. So cool."

Pete looked at Jane and tried to smile. She was so irreverent sometimes. She always made him want to laugh, but he felt he wasn't supposed to.

"They'll be valued and taken care of, Jane," Kimo said.

Pete looked down at number 72's balls. They were absurdly colossal. They encouraged him. "Hey, Kimo," he said, "were you sad when you broke it off with Sophia?"

Kimo turned off his hose. He liked to give people his full attention. In the years he had deserted their family, he'd attained this calmness and attentiveness that bugged the fuck out of Pete, especially because they were good qualities—the kind you weren't supposed to get annoyed with.

"I suppose," Kimo said. "It was a nice kind of sadness, though. The kind that makes you feel alive. Like you've done something."

"I see," Pete said. He turned to see if Jane was listening. She had a sickened expression on her face as she scrubbed the bull's ass. Pete turned back to Kimo. "Did it end right when you moved? I know it did, but I just want to make sure."

Kimo laughed and walked over to him, told him, "Yes. Dad sealed our fate. Why are you asking about it now? Look how good it all turned out."

"Yeah." Pete tried to see if Kimo was joking or not. He was not. The bull snapped its tail against Pete's cheek, stomped a hoof, and moaned.

"I think about that sometimes," Kimo said. "Dad. Fate. When he offered to buy me a ticket anywhere in the world, he knew what he was doing. He knew that freedom would straighten me out. Smart man."

Pete couldn't believe how his brother had managed to control his memories, as if even they were trainable animals. The separation had allowed for so much imagination. Instead of commenting on Kimo's selective memory, Pete made a sort of dismissive noise.

Kimo looked at him. "What was that noise?" he asked.

Pete shrugged.

"Jane often makes noises like that when she disagrees with something I say. Do you not agree upon the fact that Dad was a smart man?"

Pete wanted to say, he was a drunken man. He was an embarrassing man. He frightened Mom. He always made her cry. He made you cry. "He was smart," Pete said. "He was many, many things."

Kimo pondered this. "It seems there was resentment in that noise you made."

Pete thought: I resent you, dumb ass. Ponder that, and stop staring at me like I'm a goddamn wild horse. "Look," Pete said. "I don't store resentment towards Dad. I saw him every day. There was no need to store anything. I knew him, that's all."

"We make our choices." Kimo put his hand on Pete's shoulder, and then went back to the head of the bull.

"No, we don't," Pete mumbled, though Kimo heard him; he was staring at him. Pete noticed how nice his brother's eyes were. He was locked into them.

"Yes, we do, Pete. You can do whatever you want."

Pete looked away. He wasn't going to be hypnotized. He scrubbed the bull and the bull leaned into the brush. "I never wanted Dad's business," Pete said. "I was filling in for you. I was being the second-string son." He thought this sounded good. Second-string son.

"Please," Kimo said.

"You left me with everything," Pete said.

"I didn't leave you with everything. I just got myself out of it, and that's what you should have done, too, instead of making a martyr of yourself, instead of directing your energy into making snide comments and sassy grunts."

"Sassy grunts?" Pete asked, and then he made the dismissive noise again.

"What would you have done if you didn't take over

Tower?" Kimo asked. "Go and do that. Where would you have gone? Go there."

"I can't," Pete said. "I can't just walk away like you did."

"Yes, you can," Kimo said. "If it's making you miserable, I hereby give you permission to change, to behave in a manner you see fit."

"Thanks for your permission," Pete said.

"Don't be sarcastic. I'm being sincere, Pete. I'm trying to help you."

"You can help me by helping with the company. You can't just devastate a place, then leave it."

"I have my own life, Pete," Kimo said. "I'll help you by telling you to do what you have to do. It's what I did, and I pissed my family off, but things worked out in the end. It's not my fault you're too afraid to do the same. Be brave. Go ahead. Piss me off. Piss everyone off. Maybe it will work out in the end. Has to be better than what you have now. You hate your life."

"No, I don't," Pete said.

Kimo pointed to the bull. "Bull," he said, then he looked at Jane and nodded. She left her post to retrieve the next one.

Pete waited on the porch of the cottage for Sophia. He spoke to a horse: "I need to tell Sophia that we will be poor. We will struggle. Our child will wear used clothing. Sophia will have to wear stiff jeans."

Sophia came out of the cottage. He tried to kiss her

but she pointed to the lipstick on her lips. He didn't see why she needed to wear lipstick. They began walking to the main house for dinner. Pete watched Sophia gazing at the land. "I don't miss the beach at all," she said. "I want to be a rancher."

Pete considered her flighty desire. Last week she wanted to be a cement truck driver because she thought it would be cute. He remembered when they were younger and he told her that they weren't wealthy enough for her to be so crazy. Now, he supposed, they were. Or at least she thought they were. He wondered what would happen when he told her about his mistakes, his denial of the changing economy, his inability to foresee and adapt. She was an easygoing woman; she rarely flinched. Pete liked this. Or, Pete wanted to like this, but really he wanted her, if only for a few hours a day or even once a week, to be self-doubting and needy. Desperate-looking. In love. He wanted her to marry him.

Pete ran his hand along the wooden fence. "What did you see in him?" he asked. "What is he better at?" He was glad that Sophia didn't laugh at his question. He liked that she knew when he wasn't being funny.

"Honey," she said, "that was a long time ago. Four Sophias ago."

"Will you just tell me what he's better at now?"

"I haven't thought about it," she said.

"Think about it," he said.

She ran her fingers through her hair. "Well, he's better at physical labor, fixing things, making things work. Machines and such. He's a wealthy island redneck. Oh, but not a redneck, I suppose, because he's cerebral and introspective, well-mannered, articulate, yet I don't see why a redneck couldn't be those things."

"I'm not doing well," Pete said. "At work." He touched his abdomen and hoped she didn't see him wince.

"Everyone's having a hard time right now," Sophia said. "We're doing fine. What's wrong, really?"

He decided to tell her everything that was wrong. "Kimo upsets me. It's not jealousy. It's something else. Something simple. I don't like my brother. I don't like not being married to you. I hate the word 'girlfriend.' It's a marginal word. I don't like my job. We're not looking good, financially. And all of this is related. All of this is the same thing. Sophia?"

She was contemplating the dirt road. "Well, you have to love your brother," she said. "He's family. You have no choice. You just continue on."

But he did have a choice, and Kimo showed Pete that loving your family was not an obligation. "I think I hate him."

"Of course you do," she said.

"Will you marry me?" he asked.

"Will you not ask me that? What we have is fine."

"What do we have?" Pete asked.

She slowed her pace. "I don't know. A partnership."

"A partnership? That's something the elderly have,"

Pete said. "That sounds like something a Russian woman would say to her husband who she married for a green card!" He heard the Russian woman in his head: *Leesen, Paulie. Vat ve have iz a partnership. Das ol.*

"Pete," Sophia said, "my hormones are making me crazy. I'll have the baby and then we'll talk about what we have."

"Are you crazy? What do you mean, we'll talk? We're about to have a family here."

They reached the point in the road where they had to make a detour to avoid the goat.

"Just settle down," she said. "I'm very emotional. I ate a lot of cookie batter and then I did yoga and the batter trickled everywhere and I just need to get my body and mind in order." She gathered her damp hair into a ponytail then walked toward the fence.

"No," Pete said. "I want to go the real way."

"I don't think that's a good idea," she said.

"This way," Pete said.

Morris seemed to be waiting for them. His ears perked up and he sniffed the air.

"What's up, Morris? You like that? You going through puberty, is that it?"

"Honey, don't rile him."

"You can't get laid, is that it? Well, I get laid constantly," Pete said.

"May we use your road, Morris?" Sophia asked.

"Shut up, Sophia. I'm handling it."

The goat began to walk toward them.

Sophia turned around and headed to the fence. Pete grabbed her by the arm and pulled her back.

"We are going this way," he said, holding her.

"I like going the long way." She tried to shake free. "Ouch, Pete. For crying out frickin' loudly."

He let go of her arm as the goat got closer. He held out his arms, ready to absorb him again. It hadn't hurt that much the first time. It had only hurt later on. Pete kept this in mind.

"Oh, hell," Sophia said. "Please, Morris. Please don't hurt Pete."

"Stop reasoning with him. Just stay back."

Sophia tugged on his arm. "You know that it's a goat, don't you? He's not a symbol of something." Sophia backed away and began to run.

The goat dodged Pete and ran after Sophia. It then did what looked like a childhood prank—it nudged into the backs of her knees so that she fell backward over him and landed on her butt. He went easy on her—it actually looked as if the goat were helping her sit down. The goat did not go easy on Pete—he ran toward Pete and rammed into his side. This time Pete felt that something had definitely gone wrong in his body. Something had ruptured or split. He called out to Sophia. "Are you okay? You're okay, aren't you?"

"The baby," she said.

Kimo, Anne, and Jane ran toward them from the main house. Pete was nauseous. He cringed at the ache escalating in his center.

Kimo went to Sophia. "Don't touch her," Pete said to his brother. "You see what you did? All I asked was for you to move the goat. And now look. Sophia was almost killed."

"Yes, I was very close," Sophia said.

Pete walked to her. She was sitting up in the dirt. He was relieved all of a sudden. He had a real excuse to hate his brother now.

Kimo whispered something to Anne, and Anne approached Sophia and helped her up.

"I would know if something was wrong. Nothing feels wrong," Sophia said, her hand on her stomach. "Nothing's wrong with me, that is." She glared at Pete.

"Good," Anne said. "Let's get you to the house. We'll check you out, okay? Okay."

Jane asked Pete, "Are you all right? You look crazed."

"I'm not crazed. What are you talking about?" Pete took Sophia's hand.

"No," she said. She shook him off of her. "Just go home." She nodded toward the cottage. "I can't believe you'd do this. To prove what?"

"What?"

"Just go. Go on to bed."

"We'll take care of her tonight," Kimo said.

"And then what?" Pete asked. He noticed Jane shaking her head.

"Then, nothing," Sophia said. She let Anne put her arm around her and lead her toward the glow of his brother's home. Jane and Kimo stayed with him as if to see out his punishment.

"This is absurd," Pete said. "You did this."

"I didn't do anything," Kimo said. "Are you okay? Did you get hurt?"

Pete could feel something deep within him surfacing. A kidney. Something. It was shedding its tissues and anchors, releasing itself from its obligations and stabbing into the roof of his stomach. "No," Pete said. No one knew how hurt he was. Even Sophia thought he had just been bruised. It was his secret.

"Look what you've done to your wife," Kimo said. "Or whatever she is. She could have been hurt. Your baby could have been."

"I don't care," Pete said. "It's you." Pete jabbed a finger into his brother's chest. "You."

Kimo wouldn't duel. He was the calm, ruthless lead. Instead, as he had always done, Kimo walked away. "You've ruined my life," Pete said. "It's over." And for a moment, he wondered if it really was over. If these were the last moments of his life.

"Get a new one, then," Kimo yelled back. "I dare you."

"I hate him, too," Jane said, and then she whispered, "I'll bring you some food," before running to catch up to the dark figures of the women.

About twenty minutes later, Jane came to the cottage with a picnic basket and told Pete to follow her. They tromped through tall grasses and pockmarked mud not saying anything. Pete was so tired. He couldn't keep up and Jane kept going farther. "My appetite doesn't need to be worked up," Pete said.

"Oh, come on," she yelled back. "What's wrong with you? This is nothing."

Pete was nauseous. He couldn't get a good breath.

When they reached the farthest pasture, Jane covered the grass with a blanket and gave him his dinner, but before taking a bite she said, "You can't eat too much. You're only going to use it to disguise the taste of this." She sprinkled some dried mushrooms onto his noodles. "I picked them out of the cow shit this morning," she said. "It's my auction tradition . . . well, since last year. Have you tripped before?"

"Yeah," Pete said. "I mean, no. Shit, Jane. Literally. Shit. I can't do this. This isn't right."

"No, you're not right. That's why you're going to do this. Eat as little food as possible. Your stomach will hurt otherwise."

What would Kimo think of this? he wondered. He smiled. "What would your dad say?"

"He'd give me pebble torture."

They both laughed. Pete held his stomach. The long grass beneath him was bent over, forming a kind of cushion. The air was cold. It bit his face. He liked the cold. He liked not having a table. Pete sampled the food. Even hidden in starch and sauce, the mushrooms made him gag, much to his niece's amusement. Pete felt excited. He was finally going to let his mind go. He finished his portion and waited.

They stargazed for a while then lay on their stomachs and looked at the house bright with light. Jane said that her mom was checking out Sophia.

"How?" Pete asked.

Jane said she didn't know.

Pete flipped over, sat up, and waited for something to happen. "Now what?" he asked. "What will happen?"

"It's unpredictable," Jane said.

"Is it fun or mellow or sad or what?"

"All of that. Everything. I can't believe you've never done this before."

"I know," Pete said. "Are you feeling it yet? Am I?"

"Maybe no one will come to the auction tomorrow," Jane said. "Would that please you?"

"Hey, come on," Pete said, but he was too lazy all of a sudden to protest. He let her chastise him. How did Jane know? How did she know him so well? She was a smart girl. A smart, smart, beautiful girl. Jane was on his side. Jane was his best friend. So was the blanket. But not the moon. He hated the moon.

"You guys have that biblical brother thing going on," Jane said.

Pete looked at the mountain shining blue in the distance. Everything looked so good from far away. He would be a distant boyfriend. A distant brother. Father. Then, he would be loved. He waved at the mountain. "Whoa," he said.

"I have some ground rules," Jane said. "No interfering with animals. They don't need to see us this way, and plus, they'll bug you out. And no talking about the meaning of life and if we're just dreaming, or what is reality. I brought you out here to just observe. Don't think so much. Wow. That took an hour to say."

Pete laughed. He laughed for a while. He was teary and sniffly and long-feeling. He just felt really long. "You sound like the ranch hand. The rules."

Jane laughed. "Totally. That guy's cool."

Pete imagined this mysterious man. He was all man, sturdy on his trustful steed. Irresponsible. Charming. Dangerous. Pete wanted to be these things.

"Dad moved the goat. You won. Sophia said that. She said that you won."

"I won," Pete said. He felt a cramp springing from a deep well within him. "Jane? Will you take a look at this for me? Tell me what you think." He lifted up his shirt and showed Jane the bruise. It had yellowed, but the swelling was still there, and the odd, hard bump that he had felt was visible now.

"What is that?" Jane said.

"Feel it."

She placed a hand on his waist. Pete flinched because her hand was cold and she had pressed a bit too much.

"It could be anything," she said. "Maybe we should go back. No. We couldn't go back now."

"It could be anything," Pete said. He heard her say something more, but the words were muffled. The grass and the stars—they were drowning her out; they were making a racket. He went back to imagining the life of the ranch hand because that had been fun. He imagined that he was the ranch hand. He got on the horse and galloped, rode toward the impenetrable places. He was strong and healthy, full of rich breath. He was not hurting, not falling back onto the blanket. He was not seizing up in pain. Ride into the sun, he told his horse. To the mountain. Take me to the acres of life beyond it.

Pete opened his eyes. He was on his back, curled into a fetal position. "Sophia lost her virginity to your father. Did you know that?"

"No," Jane said. "That's messed up." He noticed her hand was still on his stomach.

"I need help," he said to Jane. "I need to go to the hospital."

She rose instantly and began to help him to his feet. So responsive, Pete thought, and she believes me; he was so grateful for that.

"We're going to get so busted," Jane said.

Pete stretched. "Why those ground rules?" he asked. A few drops of water fell from his eyes. "Why not talk about the meaning of things?" Streams of air came from his mouth as he said this. He watched the streams. There was too much going on. "Everyone needs to be able to speak at some point."

"I know," Jane said. "There's so much to say."

"We need to gather ourselves," Pete said. "Before we go back there." The grass whispered into his calves. "Why do you hate your father?"

Jane sniffled and wiped her eyes. "If I were to say, it

would just sound juvenile, so I won't say. You know how it is, don't you? He can hurt you, but in this quiet way."

"Yes," Pete said. He looked at the house and noticed that the lights were off.

"Do you feel that my dad has something over you? Because of Sophia?"

"Yes," he said. "Sophia and more. Juvenile." He wondered if they were sleeping or if maybe nobody was home. He felt angry. If something had gone wrong, he should be there. He should be included. He hated Kimo. He had no doubt about this now and no guilt.

"I feel I have nothing," Pete said. "No family, no job, no wife, no body." He looked down at his body.

"Then you're not responsible for anything," Jane said. "That could be fun." She walked a few steps, letting Pete use her as a crutch.

"I need more time," Pete said, stopping. He was so angry, so full of hate.

"Here," Jane said. She lifted her arms and gathered Pete into them. They hugged for a while in the pasture, holding each other, waiting until they felt strong enough to continue. Pete felt that he could stay in her embrace for a long time. He could live there. He felt he was lying on his deathbed and it felt okay. Jane kissed him on the cheek and then on his lips. Pete felt her tongue rolling across his. So strange, he thought.

"Why did you do that?" he asked, rolling his tongue across his teeth, his gums. It had been a while since he had been kissed like that. It was a teenage kiss. A real kiss.

"I don't know," Jane said. "Because." Jane yawned. Pete yawned. "Because I'm sad."

"Oh," Pete said.

"Because he makes me feel hurt." Tears surfaced, then spilled down her face. Pete wiped them into the night.

"Where does it hurt on you?" she said.

"Here," he said, not pointing anywhere. She held his hand. I have no family, he thought. No wife, no brother. Let the children fend for themselves. He touched her face, tried to pick up the tears with his fingertips. He ran his fingers through her hair. This is a terrible thing, he thought, but he gave himself permission. He was going to do what he wanted to do. He was going to be brave. What would happen after this, after this kiss? His insides whirled, his heart shuddered; his organs were on the loose, running wild in his body, and he put his questions aside. Jane pressed her forehead into his chest, creating an isolated heat. She lifted her face to him and they kissed again, taking their private and quiet, childish revenge.

Begin with an Outline

Setting

My dad still has the secret ranch on the Big Island. It looks like a banana plantation but it isn't. The plants don't extend very far within the ranch's perimeter. The bananas are a lie.

I am asked to reveal what I remember. I remember red dirt roads, steel gates, and signs painted with the words NO TRESPASSING. I remember the large holes in the ground, ambushes covered with blankets of grass. One of the holes was filled with sand so I could have a sandbox to play in. I remember the bananas—apple bananas, small and sweet. Lies can taste good. I haven't been to the ranch for fifteen years.

Besides the bananas my dad raises chickens and grows red ginger and marijuana. I'm not sure how large his drug operation is or how much money he makes. I know that he smokes a lot of pot, but not so much for recreational use. It's more about him testing his wares. He rolls joints. He doesn't own a bong, hookah, pipe, chillum, vaporizer, scale, dugout system, grinder, or steamroller.

I currently live in Colorado and am about to graduate from a liberal arts college where people try their best to look dirty and poor. These kids love their pot accessories and they like to make sure their apparatuses are unique. They buy pipes with unusual shapes and give them names such as the Purple Devil or the Reverend.

There are many types of potheads here—the hippie smokers out on the quad tossing Frisbees, the blunt and Old English variety sitting on porch steps, mouthing Eazy-E lyrics and dipping their heads in time to their tight, inner beat breaks. There are the wake-and-bakers, those few who roll out of bed and feed immediately, loading their devices with such ease and normalcy it's as if they're preparing a bowl of oatmeal. The most common type of smoker: the kind that lives by the clock, practitioners of the righteous 4:20 dorm room bong hit.

What kind of smoker am I? I'm none of the above. For me pot is something else entirely—it's my home, my original setting. It's my father. It could be my inherited trade. Like steel or plastics, or the blacksmith; it's all in the family. It gets passed on.

My dad used to send me samples from his plantation every now and then, reminding me he was still in business—this message via shimmering buds, hairy and fat and, beneath the brown packaging and coffee beans, seriously reeking.

Choosing a Subject

I shouldn't talk about my father. Charles Dickens tried to create a horrendous character for a novel modeled on his father. When people read the novel, they sympathized with this character. I don't want to make that mistake.

I guess I'll say that he's Hawaiian, Tahitian, Samoan, etc.—a mutt, but I won't give him a name. I guess I'll say that he no longer sends me packages because four months ago he was arrested and he currently lives in jail. The prosecutor, Allen Bernard, wants me to reveal what I remember. I tell him I remember red dirt roads.

When I was six, my mother had to leave him, admitting she needed essentials like a BMW and white leather pants. She was twenty-one and over the slumming-it stage. It was time to return to her roots, and she took me with her. We moved to Oahu and forgot.

Her name is Madeline. Maddie. She is what you would call a go-getter. She plans parties. That's her job. She focuses on details. She wraps tent poles with tea leaves. She puts glitter in the pools. Nothing is spared.

To make up for my infanthood spent in squalor, I was treated to good things—tennis camp, private school, a white Cabriolet, and a miniature horse named Rambo.

In our new life there were ladders everywhere and my mother climbed them with ease. I can't imagine her living on the ranch: my bleached blond mom in generic jeans gazing upon the fat of the plantation from her spot on top of the food chain. She says she was rebelling from her parents, but grew tried of it because they weren't watching and, using her words, "rebelling was so *unfashionable*. I always looked like an activist, or a *feminist.*"

When I ask her about our old rustic life, she tells me how cute I was, running around naked. My chore was to feed the chickens and she said I would stand on a footstool to scatter the corn so the chickens knew who was boss.

Now she is married to a strapping banker. He's heavy in the ass, a slurper of soup, and a parader of small running shorts. Hugh. He used to be an infamous lifeguard who entertained lady tourists by saving them when they weren't drowning. He was known for wearing slacks and collared shirts to the beach, and for a brief time in the late sixties the look caught on. Gucci loafers and Sex Wax. Polo shirts paired with board shorts. Hugh had influenced dress codes.

Significant Details

On Oahu, people raised restaurants instead of cattle.

My dad called me on some birthdays—my tenth, my thirteenth, and my fifteenth. The conversations were always an exercise in call and response, similar to the blues, yet without the passion and distress and only the humor and cover-up. There hasn't been a phone call in a long time. Before he went to jail there were just smelly packages with the occasional note. His last note read: *They got planes circling my property. Planes with heat detectors. I don't use heat lamps, you lolos! Keep on circling! Aloha, Dad.*

The note also said that the police were destroying his crops and that weed was decreasing in popularity due to the ice epidemic, except in his words it said, *5.0 went bus' up my goods. Locals like tweak now. Factory jobs. Pot, fo'get it.*

The prosecutor, Allen Bernard, wants me to testify against my father. I don't know all of the details, not even what he's charged with, but I know Allen Bernard isn't concerned with the crops or if my father has sent me marijuana. He wants to know what I remember about the ranch. What was it like growing up there? What did the property look like? Were there traps covered with blankets of grass? Did I ever fall into one of these traps?

Apparently a little girl wandered off from her house and fell into a very big man-made hole. My dad got her out. My dad says he wasn't aware of any holes skirting his property. He would have covered them if he knew of their existence. Allen Bernard is sure he knew of their existence.

Allen Bernard doesn't understand that I don't know my father. He doesn't understand because I'm too ashamed to tell him. He says there's no stronger bond than that between a father and a daughter and that he understands if my memory isn't "up to par." "But you know what's right and what's wrong," he says. "And you'll do what's right because you love him."

"Yes," I say. "I love him." I want to please Allen Bernard. There's something about his voice that makes me want to wear an apron and cook meat loaf constantly. I tell Allen Bernard that I'm highly conflicted and tormented. *I don't know if I remember holes in the ground. I remember the roads, the chickens. I was just a little girl.* I love our dramatic conversations. I imagine him on the other end of the phone—chestnut hair, a wad of gum on his tongue, fingers snapping at his assistant to hand him a pen. Sex-y.

"Does your father frighten you?" he once asked.

"Oh yes, Allen Bernard," I said. "Very, very much."

Regional Dialect

Since age six, I have seen my dad twice. He's like a whale that way. The year I graduated from high school was my most recent sighting. My grandmother on his side invited me to their family reunion that summer— she said it was about time I met my relatives.

At the reunion, my dad and I talked between rounds of drunken ukulele fun. He had an earring, a tattoo, and a beer. He was tan and muscled. He looked like someone I would make out with. That was weird. I asked if I could visit him and he said, "We'll see."

I asked for his phone number. He said he'd give it to me later. I wondered why he didn't want me, why he didn't invite me to the ranch. I imagined living with him—being an outlaw, being wanted. Sometimes, in my fantasies, I brought my life on Oahu along with me, and in my imagination it all worked out. My mother would be there, redecorating the ranch house, creating the illusion of more space with mirrors and bold stripes. Hugh would be there, too, adding that special yucky something, a key ingredient, like baking soda. The banker, the decorator, the drug lord, and the child. An odd, yet functional assembly line.

We ate sea urchins and opihis—creatures he plucked from reefs earlier that day.

"Why don't you want me to visit?" I asked.

"Here," he said. "I got something for you."

He searched through his backpack and brought out a jeans jacket that had a distinct eighties style, but not in a cool retro sort of way. It was obviously from the children's department, perhaps the young teen racks. I put it on. The cuffs were at my elbows. The waistband was about five inches below my boobs. I turned up the collar.

"A cropped jeans jacket," I said. "I love it, Dad." I wanted to say the word *dad*. I had never called someone that before. His effort made me so hopeful. It made me feel normal. I didn't care that the jacket was acid-washed; supplied by Sears, demanded by New Kids on the Block. I thought that this must be what families did—they bought each other bad gifts and said thank you. Thank you, Dad. I gave him a hug and pretended I was a girl with a good father. I asked for his phone number again and he squeezed me hard and began to sing. He had a falsetto voice, beautiful and steady. He sang the Queen's Prayer, a haunting, mournful song the last queen wrote in jail while the monarchy was being overthrown. I knew the English translation; in grade school we were forced to memorize it in chapel. *Forgive the sins of man,* the song said. *Your mercy is as high as heaven.*

"Why are you singing this?" I asked. Was he sending me a message?

"It's what the band's playing," he said, and I heard the faint strumming. At *Amene* we stopped hugging. Our eyes were wet. We looked away from each other. "Sad song," I said.

"Going to get a beer," he said.

I never got his number. I wasn't angry with him, though I wanted to be. It's hard to commit to logic. Logically, I should have been upset. All I have wanted, then and for some time now, is for him to want to see me. I have wanted to return to my original home, but at the reunion I wasn't angry. I was drunk. I sat at the table and looked at the food—the black lumps of boneless bodies coming out of their hard shells. I felt my own body, arms paralyzed by the unyielding jacket, my back pushing against the seams. I thought that maybe this is how life's supposed to be—nothing's supposed to be contained. Structures will stay the same, but the insides will grow and grow. Nothing will ever fit.

That night a little cousin introduced me to everyone as her auntie and kept trying to hold my hand. I walked around among the strangers, my family, thinking of liquids—the sperm that made me, his blood that's in me, the sweat on this cousin's small hand, all hidden. I had to talk pidgin or not talk at all with this side of the family in order for them to like me and not think I was some white bitch. Here's a bit of conversation:

Them: "Keolani girl, how you been? Long time no see, ah? You going go schoo on da mainlan? Ho, you smart, ah? Like Erin Brockvich."

Me (K): "Yeah."

Minor Characters
Quotations from Nathan:

"Families are like bony shoulders we're supposed to be comfortable sitting on."

"I am in love with you."

"Do you want to have sex?"

I think Nathan loves my background, but not me, necessarily. He loves the fact that I'm in pain, though I'm not sure he believes it's real. He says my desire to see my dad and return home is a "classic plot" and that he understands my "need to journey into the heart of darkness."

He wants so badly to be compelling, tries to distinguish himself by talking endlessly about Bakhtin and Foucault, Keats and sestinas. Doesn't he know that all schoolboys are impassioned by the same things—oil, Tibet, Thelonious Monk, Fritz Lang? High school boys were this way also—constantly repeating themselves, yet they were dumb and angry—masculine. But I can't love them; I have to love the Nathans because I'm growing up. Lately, at the coffee shop, I force myself to eat biscotti instead of the fudgy cookie. I have to take these small steps.

Nathan would hate this outline. He'd say that it's clever, but that gimmicks are keeping me from true emotional content. "How does this self-deconstructing form explain your emotional life?" he'd ask, and perhaps I need this voice in my head.

Quotations from Lydia Dyer:

"You're crying 'cause your dad grows herb? Shit."

"You're crying 'cause your dad won't give you his phone number? My dad used to *hit me*, okay?"

"You had a Mongoose bike and a Cabriolet. You want to know what I had? A doll made out of chicken bones."

Lydia Dyer sits in front of me and Nathan in Intergenerational Equity: Budgets, Debt and Generation X. She gives me perspective. She definitely has me trumped with the whole abuse and chicken bones thing. She is the opposite of Nathan. I believe poignancy gives her hives. Hers is another voice I like to have in my head. *Be distant,* it says. *Don't articulate the thing that's most upsetting. Allocate your scarce resources wisely; use irony, an unorthodox structure. Make it funny. This will make more sense.*

Quotations from Playwriting Teacher:

"You have great experiences to recall from."

"Take advantage of your pain."

"Do you want to have sex?"

I interpreted his advice: *Exploit pain. Become phony and superficial, indifferent like stage directions or the parentheses that contain them.*

After a while I tore up these directions. There is nothing worse than comparing tragedies, competing. He said I had misunderstood—he meant that I could create art from tragedy. I could paint, dance, act, or write it into form. Begin with an outline, he said. A blueprint, or a frame.

And then he added: "But don't write about college. No one wants to read about Life in College, and you're not going to write about *us,* are you? Don't write about us."

I told him that I wouldn't say a word, and I won't, at least in this outline. But he has given me other advice that I plan on taking one day: *Give yourself permission to say anything you want; once it hits the page, it's fiction.*

The last of the minor characters are my roommates, Tim and Jolene. They're amazing. They solve problems using hacky-sacks, ropes, and carabiners. They climb mountains as if they're apartment steps. I try to see things through their eyes—life as something to belay across. Row through. Their postgraduation plans include heli-skiing in Alaska then moving to some large city (they're not sure which one) to help homeless people.

They say, "I love you," each time they part. I scoff at them. I envy them. They take turns doing each other's laundry and buying her birth control pills. They play board games, they do fun runs, and they loved my dad's packages so I usually gave it all to them. I passed it on.

Scenes
One (Narrative Drive):

When K first gets to Colorado, she drives. She drives on icy roads. She drives on highways and over coiled passes. She reads the signs—I-25, LOVELAND PASS, LOW VISIBILITY, SNOW ROUTE. NORTH, SOUTH, EAST, WEST. These words are exotic. These are real directions. In Hawaii, it's either *mauka* or *makai*—mountains or ocean. She cannot stop driving. She can't believe that you can drive for an hour and be in a different place.

One more:

K is flying home for Christmas.

The stewardess announces that she will be passing

out pencils and scratch paper for those who want to play Halfway to Hawaii. Whoever guesses the time they'll be halfway there, or whoever comes closest, will win a bottle of champagne. The stewardess tells them the exact time they left LAX. She tells them how fast they are going and how much headwind they are receiving. She tells them the distance the flight covers, and when they are expected to arrive.

K writes down the facts. She wants to win, and she tries to remember the equations from high school. She's an econ major, for Christ's sake—she should know this. Is it distance equals rate times time? Then, to find the time, distance must be divided by rate? She doesn't know. She has no idea how headwind is supposed to fit in. Plus, she forgets about time zones.

5:27 P.M. is the answer. D12 is the winner. She can see parts of him, the winner, from where she is seated. She can see his fingers drumming a beat on the armrest. She can see the top of his head, his brown hair gelled to one side, except for one strand that points to the roof of the plane and trembles under the ventilation. When the stewardess comes by with the reward, K sees his hand grip the neck of the bottle.

"That should've been mine," K says, and the man turns to look back at her. He has good bone structure, whatever that means. He has the kind of face that winners and bankers have. K smiles to let him know she's joking. Ha. Ha. She's a funny girl. She's full of wisecracks.

"Should've, would've, could've," the man says, then turns to face forward.

K looks at her watch and waits. At 5:27, she looks out her window, and for a minute she sees what halfway looks like—ocean and air. No landmarks, nothing at rest. From the height of the plane, the ocean is calm, inviting even. But she knows that up close it would be choppy and nearly impossible to swim in. Up close it would be exhausting.

What Does She Want?

Soon I will have a piece of paper saying that I majored in economics and minored in creative writing. I don't know what I'll do with this information. I'd like to follow in my parents' footsteps. Pot growers and trophy wives are decent professions—they're practically recession-proof and they get awesome fringe benefits.

Earlier this year, before the arrest, I called my mom and told her I wanted to see him. I asked for directions home. I never asked her for his phone number before because I always wanted it to be him who gave it to me, but this time I asked. She told me she thought visiting him wasn't a good idea.

"You have a different life now," she said. "Don't you like what I've given you? What have I done wrong?"

My senior thesis explores Congress's unwillingness to apply basic economic principles to drug policy, and how ignoring economic forces will prove unsustainable over the long term. This isn't earth-shattering but I enjoy its relevance to my father's career.

I told my mother I was going to see him to claim my inheritance, my trade, and that this wasn't about who's the better parent; it wasn't about love. This was economics. This was about utilizing my B.A.

Critical Moment

But it was about love. And forgiveness. I wanted to go to my father, sit him down, and tell him that I didn't know half of me—I didn't remember the ranch; the lessons in getting by, the importance of wearing camouflage. I didn't remember how to speak as he does and I didn't want to feel like a tourist or like President McKinley when I was around his half of the family. I wanted to belong. I wanted to know that part of me. When he wouldn't let me see him, it seemed that an entire history, an entire culture, wouldn't let me in.

So here's what I wanted. I wanted access. I wanted postgraduation employment. I wanted to stand before him on my little painted footstool, evoking my old chore—feeding the birds. I'd tell him that I wanted to start from scratch and I'd say, "Should I feed the damn chickens or should I tear them apart?"

I didn't do that, of course, but I did get his number and I did call, and I'm sure that now that he needs me to be on his side, he regrets our conversation, because whenever I think about the call I think of Allen Bernard and my strong desire to please him. I think of how badly I want someone in this world to understand where I'm coming from.

Critical Answer

He said he no longer raises chickens.

He asked how I got his number.

"I'm resourceful," I said. "I'm a good worker." I prepared to launch into my Proposal. This was a big day for me; it was the day I would ask him if I could come home and it was the day I would finally get an answer.

"I sampled the last batch," I said.

"Good stuff, right?" he said.

"You should really consider growing pot that allows a functional high. You know—weed you can smoke during the day." I reminded him of the people in the factories, working longer hours. I suggested he branch out to the States, target students and professionals. "Kids here look at this stuff as if it's legendary, island lore," I said. "Why not cultivate the romance? Kona Gold, Puna Butter. These are magical words to hippies in Saabs. The money they drop on an ounce is often more than twice the price of gold."

"I only grow," he said. "Do you need money?"

I was on the deck of my apartment and Pikes Peak, a glimmering bulk of rock, was giving me courage. I had done my research. I continued: "No. I don't need money.

I want to help you on the ranch. We can get to know each other this way. I studied economics. We can teach each other things. Tit for tat or whatever. For example, I'm thinking, instead of growing plants the size of Christmas trees, we could try crossbreeding small, fast-growing plants in pots that can be quickly moved so the narcs can't pull them up."

My father didn't respond.

"We could even plant decoys," I said.

I envisioned the house, remembering it was made out of aluminum. I imagined it rusting beautifully—the blues and red-oranges against the surrounding green banana and marijuana leaves. I imagined him greeting me, stepping from a small clearing between patches of tall ferns, carrying a stalk of red ginger. His hair would smell like mud, and walking beside him to the house, every now and then I would get a punch of scent, familiar yet unfamiliar: the flat, plant scent of marijuana not yet plucked, but harvested in the wetness.

Unexpected and Inevitable

I found out I had a stepmother. She was on the phone, listening. After my last comment she said, "Stop suggesting things. You sound like one missionary. Next thing you know she going buy us out then name the ranch after herself." Click.

"Wife," my dad said. "Sorry."

"Oh," I said. "Congratulations."

"She helps me out," he said.

"Listen," I said. "I don't care about learning the business. I was just trying to find a connection. I want to visit and we can talk then. We'll talk about anything you want to talk about."

What came next is predictable. Everyone wants the person or the parent that is absent. It's the best way to be desirable, something I should have known from economics. Things are valuable when they're hard to find. Marijuana and my father are essentially weeds; if legal or easily attained they'd be less valuable than corn. My distortion of basic supply-and-demand dynamics rendered otherwise worthless crops extremely profitable. Like the drug war, I, too, provide price supports for organized crime.

"I'm glad Mom took you," he said to me. "You're smart. You got one nice house, I bet. You can be someone one day. You don't want this."

"I don't know what *this* means," I said. "Forget about my stupid pot suggestions. I just want to visit. That's all." I swallowed a pain in my throat. "What's that noise?" I asked.

"Water boiling. I'm boiling peanuts."

Boiled peanuts—I remembered eating them at the family reunion—the soft shells, the salty straw smell. The sound of the boiling made me feel breathless and pale, the gulping sound suggesting someone exhaling underwater, drowning.

"Why can I hear the water? It's so loud."

"Phone picks up background noise. Mess with recordings just in case, you know, someone went tap the line."

"Oh," I said.

"Keolani girl," he said. "You too good for this place."

"No, I'm not," I said. "It's where I'm from. Just one visit. Just one time."

"Nah," he said. "You know. The wife. Getting you here. Bumbye one hassle. Too dangerous."

My father, I realized, was breaking up with me. "You make no sense," I said. "I can barely understand your language. And my name is K. Just K."

The secret ranch. The secret rain forest. I suddenly remembered the discarded cones of marijuana, using them instead of dolls in my sandbox. I'd make the cones hold each other's stems and kiss. I'd squeeze the shampoo out of the red ginger plants and wash their rough green skin. I'd have the cones talk to each other. One would say, "I'm not happy here," and the other would say, "But it's paradise."

"Don't send me anything anymore," I said to my dad. "And don't call." I realized my mistake. I didn't have to tell him not to contact me and he hasn't contacted me since.

Now I have the power to hurt him.

I also have the power to forgive him. I think of the Queen's Prayer. *Your mercy is as high as heaven. / Behold not with malevolence the sins of man / But forgive / and cleanse.*

Denouement

I retrieve my dad's last package from my closet. I invite Tim and Jolene, Nathan and Lydia to join me in smoking the last of him. It's my big finale. It's cleansing time.

I sit next to Nathan on the living room couch. Lydia takes the recliner. Tim and Jolene sit in chairs made out of inflatable sleeping mats. They wear identical outfits—fleeces and shorts, socks and Tevas.

Like me, Nathan doesn't smoke very much, but unlike me, he has poor pot etiquette. He says, "Like, groovy, man. Like, pass the ganja," and he coughs for so long it scares all of us.

"Your dad's awesome," Tim says. "Did he go to career day at your school?"

Everyone laughs. Nathan sounds like a sheep bleating. A stoned sheep bleating.

No one knows he's in jail. No one knows I could help to keep him in there.

"Oh my God," Nathan says. "Show them the yearbook."

"No," I say.

"Come on," Nathan says.

Nathan always urges me to resist humor, and now he's urging me to get the yearbook. He's insisting on funny.

I get the yearbook and return.

It's my mom's yearbook from her senior year of high school. I turn to her glossy, dreamy photograph. Her eyes sparkle; her blond hair is ironed straight. She wears a dress stamped with bold floral prints and a puka shell necklace. Every senior picture floats above a statement, a quote meant to illustrate the person you are or the person you want people to think you are. A saying to encapsulate you in 1972. The girl next to my mother—her statement says:

> *I'd like to teach the world to sing in perfect harmony. I'd like to hold it in my arms and keep it company.* —New Seekers.

The quote under my mother's senior picture reads: *I've got a book of matches.*

"It doesn't make sense without him," Nathan says, and he flips through the pages and points to my dad. My dad wears a stiff palaka shirt and a puka shell necklace. He looks so strong and young, ready to pounce right out of the pages and into real life. The quote under his picture: *Come on baby light my fire.*

It shocks me every time. They don't seem to be my parents. They could be my friends, a couple like Tim and Jolene or me and Nathan, young and childless. I glance up and everyone is laughing silently, and I feel ashamed.

"You know they were stoned when they wrote that," Lydia says. "They were totally high."

Epiphany

I think about my mother's beautiful house, my bedroom and its glass sliding door with wood trim. Every morning, I would wake to the sound of chattering birds and the looming greenness of the mountain range upon which battles between Hawaiian tribes were fought. On my four-poster bed, I'd inhale the scent of lychee bleeding through the wire screen behind the wooden jalousies. I would walk to the kitchen where a woman named Lehua would be making me breakfast, and I'd have trouble looking at her. This is where I belong. This is the place I love. His half of me is gone.

It's not so much an epiphany as an admission of guilt. I do not have any other major insights or overwhelming feelings; the sky does not assume a white radiance; my soul does no slow swooning, and generous tears do not fill my eyes as I contemplate my failed attempts at merging my two halves into one. This merge seemed more critical than the decision I have to make now. Hurt him or help him? Was my father aware of the pits skirting his property? Well, yes, he dug them, of course. Do I remember falling?

I imagine the other little girl at the bottom of the hole. He could have buried her. That's what the holes are for. I wonder if she saw earthworms squirming through the walls, if she rested on the bed of grass and looked at the sky and the passing clouds, a drifting plane. I wonder if she held her pee or if she let it go. I wonder if my father hesitated at all or if he saved her right away and brought her home without thinking of the consequences. He saved me; or rather, he got me out of the hole he made. He didn't find me until it was dark and I was very afraid.

My mother told Allen Bernard she remembers me having nightmares about falling into a hole. She didn't tell him anything else. She has left it up to me.

What happens to my father? Will I testify against him? What do I write in? What do I omit? Will I keep telling this story, in one form or another, over and over again?

I just want someone to understand me. I just wanted to visit.

I look outside at Pikes Peak, the falling sun, the sunset swept over the mountain. Reds and oranges, bruised yellows, dark silver clouds. The sky looks like rusting aluminum, like bananas—small sweet lies. This is as close as I'll get to his home, my home, a place I truly don't remember that well, Mr. Bernard, but I hope this outline helps.

Secret Clutch

When Noe asked him to help zip her up, Kent wormed his finger into the thin folds of fabric over her lower back, found the small metal handle, then followed the silver, toothy trail, the silk swallowing the dress's metal ridge. He tried not to look at her back, smooth and curved like a violin. He tried not to look at the black beauty mark on her shoulder, a swirl of pigment like a notch in wood or a drop of shoyu on brown rice. He focused on the zipper's grooves lined up like soldiers, each one essential in holding something together. He thought of teamwork and duty.

Her dress. In the wind the fabric seems to lap up the air around her. In the wind the silk presses against her skin and you can see the outline of her body, its swells and flats, muscles and bones. Her dress is magenta. Noe is Kent's nanny. Kent is sixteen.

.   .   .

Tonight is the Fourth of July and they are now at his mother's wedding reception, which is at her and her new husband's home on Wailaiʻiki Ridge. The yard is shaped like a broom, a triangular expanse of grass with a long handle of ledge that hovers over a valley. Kent and Noe stand on the handle in the wind. They float above the valley and the black and wrinkled sea.

Kent surveys the yard, the people by the bar and under the tent, which is made of sails and is staked to the ground with bamboo poles. "I need to get back to work," he says.

Kent has given himself a mission and calls it Mission Imbecile because that was what he once was: an imbecile, and he doesn't want to be one any longer. He has finally seen the light. He thought his stunts were so clever and shocking but, as his grandfather said, he was just another dim-witted participant in the great island tournament of pleasure. Now, in honor of his recently deceased Gramps, he is looking to add something new to his life. He wants to add some dignity. He wants to engage in mental combat always and forever. Most of all, he wants to show Noe that he has the potential to become a responsible man.

"Let's get this over with," Noe says. "There's Mr. Wong."

Her hair is black like charcoal. Her hair is his fuel. Kent walks toward his victim. Mr. Wong owns a chain of crack seed stores that Kent has stolen from. He loved the wasabi peas and the dried, crinkly plums soaking in li hing sauce. He'd reach his hand into those glass jars, in the thick juice, and then he'd run out of the store with a handful and jump on the Express 27 that always came to the corner of Koko Head and Wilhelmina at 3:22.

Mr. Wong sees Kent and raises both of his hands as if it's a stickup, then makes a tiny bow and laughs.

"How are you doing this evening?" Kent asks.

"You like my treats," Mr. Wong says. "You take." He presents a package of dried shredded mango from his pocket and pushes it into Kent's hand.

"No," Kent says. "I would like to apologize for my old ways," but Mr. Wong is backing away before he can continue with the spiel. He is smiling, amused, as the others were. Kent is becoming more disappointed with each response. It's as if he's going from door to door and nobody's home. To others, his desire to lead a noble life isn't admirable; it's adorable, irrelevant. Earlier this evening he apologized for ages thirteen and fourteen to the Sigfrieds, the Richardsons, and the Johnstons, people from his dad's neighborhood. He rode the Sigfrieds' mini-horse to the Circle K. While the Johnstons were away in Sun Valley he had their pool drained and used it for skateboarding, and he taught the Richardsons' parrot how to say, "My nads are on fire." All three families accepted his apology immediately. Mrs. Sigfried told him that divorce could be hard on children. Mr. Richardson said that Joshua snorts painkillers and that Kent looked like Father Damien next to his sorry sack of skin of a son.

Gramps gave Kent this apology mission about a year ago when he and Noe first moved into Gramps's house on Diamond Head. They moved in after Kent received straight C's on his report card, even a C in Glass Blowing, but Kent was a different person back then and he ignored his grandfather's various tasks, ignored all of his prescriptions that would help kill the wise-ass within.

His grandfather was a flyer in the Korean War. Kent wants to be like him, though not look like him. His teeth were different shades of khaki, though he only smiled when he saw Mrs. Sees on a chocolate box. He'd see her picture, smile, and say, "I bet she was a real good girl." In his grandfather's later years, he grew puffy and neckless. He had scattered discs of liver spots on his bald head and his left arm from sticking it out the window as he drove, and the spots were always bathing in a petroleum-jelly-like substance. Gramps looked like Jabba the Hutt if Jabba were to undergo gastric bypass surgery, yet Kent would rather resemble him than his other male role model, his handsome father, because his father is a reckless pervert. Kent has seen videotapes of him having sex with women, and the women in the videos don't look conscious. They look as if they're sailing the high seas—listing back and forth, their faces pale and vacant with motion sickness. Kent has also seen his father having sex live. Twice, he caught him in the living room. He never got to see the woman's face—just her tan leg draped over his father's shoulder and his father heaving into the body as if attempting to break down a locked door. He overheard the woman saying to his father that he makes her feel like a cavewoman, and then she made a roaring sound.

Girls are fond of Kent, too. He has been kissed, groped, and dry-humped on numerous occasions, but during these moments he always thinks of his father, and of his inner caveman, and his dick droops like a Dali watch.

What kind of man do I want to be? Kent thinks about this a lot ever since his grandfather died. What kind of man am I now? He looks at Noe's face, her body, and then his shoes. He allows himself to imagine her nipples before putting on his metaphorical coat of armor. He wonders if he has the same thoughts as his father, the same fantasies of swiveling hips and nipples with craters and hills like the surface of the moon.

When have these thoughts surfaced? And why? Why when she's around is the Dali watch replaced by something Swiss and steadfast? His dear nanny—with him since he was seven years old. Kent summons the troops, his men, his boys, to see him through these desperate times. The troops help him wage war against mental fatigue, but they're not coming. They don't have time for this. They don't understand the nature of their relationship, how she needs him but doesn't know it. They don't understand that these are their last days together. Soon, she will go. She says he doesn't need a nanny. Oh, but he does. He does. She says she's considering other offers— she's a practical and savvy woman—and he needs to prepare for her imminent departure. Oh, but he can't. He won't.

Who's next?" Noe asks. "Who else have you robbed or insulted?" She takes a pull from a longneck beer bottle. "I feel like insulting someone."

Kent puts his arm around her. "Cheer up," he says. Poor Noe. Her engagement to Racer McNaughton has been broken. Racer is a beach volleyball player, a grunting jock, a pro asshole. He's also a sugarcane heir, a literal sugar daddy. Like her predecessor, Noe didn't get to upgrade. Noe is a descendant of the Scottish-Hawaiian Princess Victoria Kaiulani, the princess who never got to be queen because the monarchy was overthrown and she died of disease and heartache. Kent knows everything about Princess K. because of Noe—she clings to her heritage because she thinks that it somehow makes her royal, but Kent has trouble reconciling her bloodlines with her profession. She's a nanny and a Tahitian dancer—she wears bras made out of coconuts and she shakes her ass while the male dancers around her waggle their tongues and swallow fire. There's nothing regal about it. Poor Noe.

Tonight, he'll have to apologize to her as well for what he has done and for what's about to happen.

"You should get drunk," Kent says. "I'll drive home."

"Yeah right," she says.

His grandfather banned Kent from any kind of vehicle including golf carts. Kent is reminded of Russell Clove and scans the area for him. Kent spots him and tugs on Noe's wrist. They walk toward Russell, who unfortunately is with his daughter, Brandy, a senior at Kent's high school and a constant presence at family functions. Kent hesitates. Brandy is sulky and skinny—a walking rib. She's also very cool. When she talks it sounds as if she's simultaneously yawning. Kent doesn't bother with formalities. He recites his memorized speech so that it will be a proper apology:

"Sorry, Mr. Clove, for ruining your golf game with my foolish antics. Like a moth to a flame I was drawn to destruction and tomfoolery." Kent looks over at Noe and she's mouthing parts of the speech along with him in a mocking way. "By chasing you and your party into the pond with my cart I was fulfilling my need for attention since my parents didn't give me any." Kent pauses. Russell is looking at him with a smile on his face as if Kent's telling a joke that's about to reach the punch line. He doesn't look at Brandy, knowing that she'll kill his flow. He's embarrassed, but reminds himself that the new Kent need not be embarrassed. The new Kent does not care for peer approval, nor does he dig through cow manure for magic mushrooms or make mustaches out of pubic hair and offer them to the drama dorks to use in their musicals. He is not like his father, he is like Gramps, and the only thing that can be depended on is his own brute strength. He will not be a pervert. He will not mistreat people because he knows what it's like to be discarded. He will recite his speech. Still, with the hope that Brandy won't be able to hear him, he mumbles the next line: "I'm now in a better environment and am on my way to becoming an upstanding citizen."

"Christ!" Russell yells. He elbows his daughter. "Did you get all that, honey?"

"Whoa," she says. "Scary."

Kent knows he's dead at school on Monday. Brandy will tell her crowd all about his apology, a crowd he once aspired to. She hangs with the mushers—skaters and stoners whose girlfriends manage to look hot in baggy clothes and DC shoes. However, Brandy is a poser and wouldn't want her sticky friends to know about the glam parties she attends. Tonight she wears a turquoise dress slit up the side of her leg and she carries the exact purse Noe coveted when she dragged him to Neiman Marcus last Saturday: the Murakami Louis Vuitton. There was no way Noe could ever afford it. How he loathes this purse. Everywhere he looks he sees it, its fluorescent logos, the white leather, women cradling it as if it's a newborn. He sees Noe nod at the purse. Brandy looks at Noe's purse, vintage Chanel, given to her by Kent's father, and nods. *Hello, Louis. Why, hello, Chanel.*

"Didn't you get suspended from the club?" Brandy asks, laugh/yawning into her dad's shoulder.

Kent knows that she knows very well that he got suspended for his antics on lobster-and-a-movie night when he went from table to table imitating the scream a lobster makes as it burns and drowns. Everyone laughed as they dunked their slabs into their tins of drawn butter, but that was months ago when he was still on the thorny path. Does Brandy want to partake in a little game of "Didn't You?" Oh, he'll play. Rumors have her putting chicken salad on her pussy and Chad Nikolai licking it off.

"Are you sniffing glue or something?" she asks.

"Oh, real clever," Kent says, then flicks his tongue and tells her there's chicken yakitori by the bar if she gets a hankering for some bird. After this, he immediately says: "Sorry."

"Whatever," Brandy says. "I don't even know what you're talking about."

"Kent," Russell says. "You did that when you were ten years old. I've gotten over it. It's dinner-party material now. It's great."

"Please, Russell," Noe says. "Just say you accept his apology. The boy has gotten into a lot of trouble and he's trying to amend his wrongs in honor of Gramps—one of the steps is apologizing."

"Oh, sure," Russell says. "I had to do that once. Twelve steps."

"I only have nine," Kent says. "I don't have to carry

my message to others and I don't have to seek through prayer."

"Decided to pass over the God parts," Russell says. "Not bad. But what about steps two, and five, six, seven?"

"You sure know your steps," Noe says.

Russell looks down at his cocktail and shrugs.

"I still have those steps," Kent says, "except instead of 'God can restore,' 'Admit to God and others,' it's 'Gramps can restore,' 'Admit to Gramps and others.' That was my grandfather's idea, but now that he's gone I guess I don't really have those steps either. Stop staring at me, Brandy."

"Well, Mr. Halford ran a tight ship," Russell says.

"I've run amok for almost sixteen years," Kent says.

"Well, amen, soldier. Over and out!" Russell salutes and shakes his glass then moves along with his slouching daughter, the collapsed rib. Brandy looks back at him and smiles. It seems genuine.

Kent closes his eyes. He loves the sound of cocktails. The clinking of the cubes sounds like the muted bells in a stuffed animal's belly. He would like a Bombay Sapphire up with a twist, but knows his taste for gin martinis comes from his father. He's annoyed by Russell's salute; it was meant to mock his grandfather, whose past as a fighter pilot has become amusing just as Noe's heritage has become irrelevant and meaningless. Even Kent is guilty of laughing at his grandfather's history, perhaps because he could never quite see it, could never envision his grandfather up in the sky working the controls of his F-86 with a smooth arm free of sores. Kent said, "My ass," when his grandfather claimed a novel was based on his troop's battle with MIGs over the Yalu River. He and Noe laughed almost uncontrollably as they browsed through a book published in 1942 called *Killing with Your Bare Hands*, where a few moves his grandfather invented can be found. Lately, Kent reads the book and he doesn't laugh. He reads the directions and looks at the drawings and diagrams of the fighting soldiers carefully as if they're the very tools that will protect him throughout his life. He even thinks about the moves, fluid as ballet, when the book is nowhere near. Now, for instance, as he sees his father by the bar, he envisions the Donkey Kick. In his mind his father is lying on the ground. *One: Take a flying jump, drawing your bent legs up to your chest and keeping your feet together. When your feet are around eight inches above your enemy's body, shoot your legs out straight, driving your boots into his body, and kill him. Two: If enemy doesn't expire and he rolls away, seize his hand and lift so he is lying on his side, slightly elevated. Apply pressure on the back of his hand and wrist. Jerk up on the arm while simultaneously smashing his lower ribs with your boot and kill him.*

At night before bed, Kent reads the passages aloud, falling asleep with the images of the pencil-drawn men fighting in his head. He can see them now, his troops— the hats like the shells of turtles, their white socks and firm faces. He sees the thrust of hamstrings, the limp wrists.

These men are his allies. He's not just honoring Gramps by trying to reform himself; he's trying to escape the holding cell of family and island because they're turning him into a bad man. Ever since he felt the twitch between his legs, he felt his hormones being pulled by genetic strings, and feared the apple was about to fall right next to the tree. These men are helping him change history.

"I need a drink," Noe says, "and an eight-ball and a pistol."

"Stop it, Noe," Kent says. "You're lucky. Beach volleyball is the pansiest sport ever." Kent thinks of volleyball men compared to the men in the *Bare Hands* book. In their illustrated diagram they'd be wearing Oakley sunglasses, fluorescent tank tops, and their legs would be hairless. They'd be in the air, backs arched, trying to spike a ball. A dialogue bubble would float above their heads and it would say, "Go Team Tanning Booth." He wishes Noe could be content with just him. The only benefit of his grandfather's death is that he and Noe get to live in his house alone and Kent feels as if they're a married couple. He wants to show her how this setup can work forever. She says that when they're done arranging his grandfather's things, she'll go, and so he assigns more chores, finds more shirts that need to go to the Salvation Army, invents new disposal and distribution conflicts. He doesn't want her to go. He loves giving her money for groceries. It's the most romantic thing ever. He doesn't want to move in with his mom and her new husband, Kula. He knows Kula won't see the purpose of a nanny since he grew up without hired help, a concept that is strange and very sad to Kent. Who bathed him? Sang to him? Tumble-dried his pajamas right before bedtime? He knows Kula is a man who'll try to bond with him through car-washing or weed-picking or football-watching because that's what families do on shows like *Roseanne*. Kent is secretly happy that Racer dumped Noe. If she had married him, she'd be a person who'd eventually hire her own nanny. She would go to the same parties as Kent, yet would actually be a real guest. He would have nothing over her.

"I'm not lucky," Noe says.

"He shaves his chest," Kent says.

"So what?" Noe says. "He was somebody. I need somebody. Do you know how easy things would have been? Of course you know. I'm not lucky. These people are lucky. This is how the West was won and all that." She lets out a very long burp.

"What would the princess think?" Kent says.

"The princess is dead," she says.

Kent wishes he could make her feel good just as she has made him feel good all his life. She has seen him cry, wet the bed, and have a tantrum. She has held him until he has fallen asleep. She has taken him to doctors, paddling practice, beaches, parties, school, concerts, outer islands, and New Hampshire, where he almost went to boarding school.

"He never even apologized," Noe says. "Not even a simple 'I'm sorry.'"

"Forget about him," Kent says, remembering the apology he needs to make to her. If he were to resemble his father, he would rub her back and let his hand knead lower and lower down the grade of her skin toward the dip above her ass. But he is not his father. He pats her back two times. Thump. Thump.

Kent breaks. He orders a drink, a Henrietta, lots of juice, little vodka. He tells the bartender how to make one. "Only top-shelf," he says, "or else I'll get sick."

The bartender looks at Noe, trying to convey a look of solidarity. Wrong move. Noe hates when workers do this, especially when she's dressed so nicely—it's as if she's a spy and her identity has been exposed. She doesn't believe she has anything in common with them—the housekeepers and bartenders, the yardmen and ironing ladies.

Kent feels guilty for drinking the vodka, but he can't help himself. He takes a deep inhalation, getting a good sniff of tuberose and smoke, prepares to apologize to his dearest Noe. A simple "I'm sorry." She has her hair swept up, piled on her head like a crown, tendrils spilling down her face. She is talking to Carl, one of Racer's "buddies," who plays polo at Waimanalo Field and walks around as if his body were not a body but a Ferrari. Carl swipes the corners of his mouth when he looks at girls.

Kent turns to the bar for a refill and there's Brandy.

"You want to dance, psycho?" she asks.

Noe laughs at whatever the pecker is saying to her. She throws her head back.

"Of course," Kent says.

They walk toward the square tile of the dance floor.

"Are you sure you haven't been sniffing glue?"

Kent shakes his head. "You know, Brandy, that's something a popular teen would say in a movie about popular teens who are later humiliated by the uncool, harassed teen at the homecoming dance."

"Random," Brandy says.

Kent doesn't point out that "random" is an overused word. "Haphazard," he says.

"What?" Brandy says. "You're so random."

On the dance floor, a slow Elton John ballad plays and Brandy holds Kent far from her body. She grips the top of his shirt with her thumbs and pointer fingers as if he's wet laundry. He pulls her in close and sings into her ear because he knows girls hate that.

"So, you're an alcoholic?" she asks.

"No," he says. "Attentionholic. Destructionholic. Tomfoolery. Holic."

A fast song comes on and more people move onto the floor. The song is from the seventies, an arrangement of toots and whistles and a single catchphrase. Kent points his finger to the sky then to the floor. Brandy hugs herself and wiggles.

"What's your vice?" he asks. Chicken salad, he thinks. So unsanitary, and yet so health-conscious.

"The usual," Brandy says. "Do you like your new stepfather?" She jumps in place and rolls her head from side to side. Her small boobs bounce aggressively. He wants to hold them still. Kent tries to make up for her lack of groove talent by leaning into a backbend, one palm on the ground, his other arm in the sky, and then he switches. Back and forth, back and forth. He has never thought of it that way before—Kula as stepfather. It's vaguely threatening. Kula is very handsome. Women slap his chest when speaking to him. Kent swoops his upper body up to a standing position in one graceful and fluid move he calls the Protractor. "I guess he's all right," Kent says.

He sees Kula on the dance floor with his mother. Kula is in a lunging position and his mother straddles one of his legs and dances over it. It upsets Kent. He waves to get her attention, then stands still, forms his lips into a Jaggerian pout, puts a knuckle on his hip, and holds out his other hand and wags a finger. Then, keeping his legs hip-width apart, Kent hops toward Brandy, and when he reaches her he thrusts his hips into her hips repeatedly while punching his fist into the sky. His gaze wanders back to his mother and new stepfather, but he sees they aren't looking at him. Instead, everyone is looking at them. Kula is really commanding the dance floor, utilizing the entire space. Kent soon realizes that Kula knows how to tap-dance. Toe, toe, heel, heel. Toe, toe, heel, heel—all the while doing the breaststroke with his arms, and then he spins. Stops. Spins. Stops. During this whole routine Kent tries to smile, but all he can think is: He's Kula than you.

Brandy's pumping her hips back into his. He feels nothing, and looks around to see where Noe is. It seems one can do things on a dance floor that would be impossible to do anywhere else. At school, for example, Brandy wouldn't be backing into him, carving circles with her butt in the space so close to his privates. On a dance floor he could put his arms around Noe and sway with her. She could nuzzle her face into his neck and cry; cry about her losses—Racer and Gramps and the monarchy.

"I see the way you look at your nanny," Brandy says. "I think you have issues."

"You don't even know me, bird lady," Kent mumbles. "I need another drink."

They leave the dance floor and walk to the bar. Kent orders two Henriettas. "She invented this drink," he says.

Brandy takes a sip. "Wow. That's the chronic."

Kent shakes his head. "Um, yeah, that's not going to work for me."

"The bomb," she says.

"Well, no."

Brandy tries again: "This drink is retarded."

"Done," Kent says. "See, the teen-movie genre has left us with little to say. Those words aren't ours anymore. Just as the rainbow belongs to the gays and Cristal belongs to the rappers."

"And the issues belong to the Kent," Brandy says. "Aren't you a little old to have a nanny?"

"No," Kent says. "Well, maybe."

"What does she do? Tuck you in?"

"No," Kent says. "We're just good, intimate friends. She cries on my shoulder and we plan the weekly menu. Her fiancé broke up with her."

"Sucks," Brandy says.

"You what?" Kent says, and then adds: "Sorry." Reformation is much harder than he thought it would be. "Josh has a nanny," Kent says. "It's not so strange."

"Josh is stupid," Brandy says. "And she's his P.A."

"Your friend Misha has a nanny," Kent says.

"Misha's a whore. And you're supposed to call them P.A.'s after you turn ten or something."

"Why do you care what I do?" Kent asks.

"Because we see each other all the time," Brandy says. "We're going to see each other for the rest of our lives since we're family friends, inheritors of the social scene."

"That is such a stupid thing to say."

"But it's true," she says. "It's all set. Your apologies made me realize we should be friends and give back to the community and stuff. We're going to do that eventually anyway."

"What the hell are you talking about?" Kent asks. "I'm apologizing to show Gramps and Noe I'm reliable, that I could be a hard worker, a provider."

"Jeez, rip me a new one. I thought you were doing your little acts of contrition because you cared what people, the community, thought of you."

"I don't care what anyone thinks of me," Kent says.

"Okay, Kent. You don't care and I love Ross Dress for Less. Glad we can be honest with each other."

Kent doesn't know what to do with Brandy's sudden interest in him and their status and future as family friends. He wants to ask the soldiers: "Do I care? What is beyond the island tournament of pleasure? Where would I go?" He sees his father talking to Noe on the ledge of the yard, the diving board of doom. Kent needs to rescue her. Who knows what his father is suggesting, insinuating, or pantomiming? There is another woman on the ledge, too. His father is probably proposing a threesome.

"Brandy, I'm going to go talk to my dad," Kent says.

"Can I come?" she asks.

Oh, the variety of ways he can answer that question. The old Kent could think of many, but the new Kent takes a deep breath, thinks of his troops, and says, "Yes, you may accompany me," and they walk toward enemy lines.

"Real tough luck, kid," his father is saying to Noe. "You could have got a lot of land in that marriage deal. Talk about reparations. Hey, son. What's the haps?"

"Hi," Kent says.

"You all right? You need therapy or anything? You like your second papa?"

"Yes," Kent says. "I love him."

His father squints. "Kula," he says. "Not so sure about a guy who's named after a place. What if I named you Latvia?" His father rocks on his heels, something he always does after he says something he thinks is funny.

"Better than naming your son after yourself," Kent says.

"Hey, watch you mouth, Kent part two. This is my new girl. I'm taking her for a test-drive. Kent. Marie."

"Pleasure," Kent says. "Pleasure me. Ting you." He cannot control himself. He hates her already because she's carrying that damn purse; it's a purse that allows him to see into a woman's mind and the view is always the same: fluorescent brain matter, different colors for different sections. Frontal lobe: orange. Hypothalamus: pink. And instead of a color for the part of the brain that does math, there's just the floating equation $1 + 1 =$ Poodle.

Marie smiles at Kent, then looks at Brandy's accessories. Kent speaks softly to his father so Brandy won't hear. "I'd like you to meet my girlfriend." He turns and grabs Brandy, who's peering over the edge of the cliff. "Dad, you know Brandy Clove, Russell's daughter."

Kent realizes his mistake. His father is giving Brandy the sex eye. The last time Kent saw the sex eye rear its sexy head was at Sunset Grill, where a woman passed by their booth and nodded at his father. After a few minutes his father explained that she was a girl of his youth, a kind of girl every man should be with before getting married because she returned favors with road head. "My car insurance wasn't the only thing that went up, know what I mean," he said.

Kent looked at his calamari steak—a tissue of pearl-colored meat bathing in a velvety yellow pulp, and pushed it aside. He was disgusted, then further disgusted at being disgusted by sex. He knew his father was ruining him. Later that evening Kent went to the turnabout at the Elks Club, jumped on an old lady's hood as she waited to merge into traffic. He pulled down his shorts, giving her a moonlit view of his ass, and then he bent over, cupped his butt cheeks, and spread them apart, giving her a different view altogether.

I'm so sorry, he says to the lady now, hoping the message will reach her telepathically. She was so old, nearing the end of her life. It was something no one should have to see, but especially her, a nice lady with a basic purse, a lady who looked like Mrs. Sees. So sorry, Kent thinks. He remembers the shirt she was wearing. Its cuteness haunts him. I'M NOT AGING, I'M MARINATING.

"How old are you now?" his father asks Brandy.

"Brandy's hungry," Kent says. "We're going to get some sushi. She has a ravenous appetite. Noe, will you come with us, please?"

"Have fun, kids," his father says. "Noe, you remember what I said. You think about it, okay? Like old times."

"Sounds like a good deal," Noe says, smiling.

Kent's face throbs with anger. What did his father say to Noe? What does she have to think about? A threesome? In the distance, between tiers of plumerias, he sees Kula feeding his mother cake. They walk toward the sushi bar and Kent has the urge to feed Noe a roll. He wants to see salmon eggs glistening on her tongue, green wasabi oozing down her chin. Brandy says she's going to get another Henrietta but Kent doesn't respond to her. He is pissed off, but before he can ask Noe what his dad was talking about he sees his mom stumbling toward the direction of the stage and he is paralyzed. Help me, Gramps, he thinks. Help me, soldiers.

Noe is also watching the stage. People are tapping their glasses with their spoons and the night begins to ring. Kent closes his eyes and pretends that there is no one here and that his mother will not make an announcement that he'll have to apologize for. But the men have heard him and they come marching through his mind with their turtle hats and delicate black shoes. They demand he pony up. One says that he didn't defeat the Shanghai terrorists and demoralize the Nazis so Kent could fiddle the PlayStation. One lists the arteries he has punctured with a knife: brachial, carotid, radial, subclavian. "Now find the Smatchet within you," the soldier says. "Admit your mistakes, or get left behind."

"Noe," Kent says. "Beloved, royal Noe, I love you."

She turns to face him. Her waist turns to face him as well. Her mini-waist, the mini-hipbones like holstered guns.

"Don't be angry," he says. "I'm just a poor kid who wanted to please his mother because she doesn't like me. Never has. Never will, but I still try to please her even though she once confided to you that being an unfit mother was 'in.'"

Noe snaps her fingers.

"I volunteered your Tahitian services."

"You what?"

"When my mom asked if you'd dance, I said nothing would give you more pleasure than to dance the dance of your ancestors."

"You're sick."

"I'm sorry," Kent says. "Like a moth to a flame I really fucked up. Come on," he says. "Who's the nanny?" He pokes her ribs. He rocks on his heels. She slaps the back of his neck, something Gramps always did to both of them. The slap makes them both pause in remembrance of someone who cared for them and tried to change their lives. When he once told Gramps he loved him, Gramps said a man should only say that to another man when he's taking his last breath. Gramps died in his sleep.

"Ladies and gentlemen, thank you for joining us tonight."

Noe looks toward the dance floor. "Bastard," she says.

"Hey, now," Kent says.

"Shut up," Noe says. "Not one word. I can't believe you would do this to me. Actually, I can."

Kent's mother thanks various people who have flown

in. She thanks her father may he rest in peace and she thanks Kula's family. She thanks her trainer. She thanks the academy. Everyone laughs. Kent waits for his thanks. He wants his mom to love him. So many of the ideas for the wedding came from him—the type of bouquet: hydrangeas and vendella roses tied with grass, a simple coconut cake drizzled with the same rose petals from the bouquet versus the fussy cake his mother initially wanted, one with pearl borders, detailed Victorian scroll, handmade drapes, and sugar-paste flowers. For party favors he suggested the valets put air fresheners in everyone's car that had his mother and Kula's image on them. Second wedding. Kitsch over sentimentality. He read all of this in *Star Weddings*.

"She better not introduce me as the nanny," Noe says.

"Noe," his mother says, "come on up here. Everyone, we have a special treat for you tonight. I want all the men to gather on the dance floor, ladies, too. Noe is going to teach us how to dance Tahitian. Loosen those hips and give thanks to the goddess of love."

"Goddess of love?"

"She meant sun," Kent says. "Father of life, right? See, I listen. Please, Noe. I promised her. I couldn't let her down."

"Sure," Noe says. "You're the boss."

The bongos begin to play and Noe walks to the dance floor. Kent follows her. This will be his last crime, he vows. He feels badly, yet he loves to watch her dance. Like a pro, as soon as she hits the magic tile, she smiles and pops her hips from side to side. Her upper body remains motionless, arms spread out, fingers pushing against the air, and she smiles so sweetly, so widely.

"Everyone, follow me," she yells. "Right, left, right, left, then speed it up. Shiver."

She begins to move her hips in tiny circles, and then the drums go wild and she goes faster while weaving herself around the men. "Figure eights," she yells. "Varu. Te huʻe nane."

"Look at that," his father says.

Kent turns to look at him. "She's really good, isn't she?" he says proudly.

"Man, I wish she'd dance like that, but under me."

Kent frowns. His father is hypnotized. He begins to swivel his hips and then he steps onto the dance floor. Kent almost reaches to grab his sleeve, but then he hears something he has never heard before.

"Thank you, Kent," his mother says. She rests her hand on his back for four seconds. "This just makes the men wild."

"It's not meant to," he says.

"Oh, yes, it is," she says.

Men have surrounded Noe. Even Mr. Wong dances, lifting one leg, then the other, then clapping twice. His father is trying to break through the wall of bodies to get to her. Noe has a lotion for every part of her body. Elbow lotion. Hand lotion. Leg lotion. Under the lights she glistens, whereas his dad has taken on a soggy look. Kent watches as he wipes his brow and flicks the sweat over the heads of others. Kula is dancing, too, but he is really Tahitian-dancing. His feet are together and his knees scissor open and closed.

"Men, look at Kula," Noe says. "That's pa'oti."

Kula does some other moves and Noe comments on them. He kicks and moves his fists. "Tu'e," Noe says. "The Horo. The Otaha. Ladies, it's as if you're sitting in a chair. Get low. Draw arcs. We're saying how happy we are in this climate."

Kent scans the swaying bodies. He sees Brandy dancing. He sees Mr. Clove making wide circles with his hips as if he's working a hula hoop while standing on a tight rope. A gap opens and his father enters, shimmying his shoulders and spinning in circles.

"Ready, Kent?" his mother says. "Your other idea is about to go off."

Kent smiles, remembers the fireworks. He had to beg her for them and justify their necessity. He asked her to imagine petals of fire covering the entire sky above the wedding party. Now he hears the explosion of the Bada Bangs, and then he sees the aerial repeaters, the spray of the palm shells dripping down the night sky. He watches the guests as they look up and see something larger than them. Then he recognizes the whine of Pyrotechnic Pandemonium. Comets burst forth, the cylinders shooting out radiant messages, then drooping like the branches of weeping willows. The dancers croon, and those who aren't dancing stare at the sky even when the sparks fade; they keep their eyes on the

exact same blank spot, waiting for the next bright um-
brella of light.

Kent knows what the final firework will be because
he choreographed the entire sequence. The night's
zenith is Operation Retribution, a sixteen-shot, five-
hundred-gram aerial repeater that shoots up red, white,
and blue sparks, then produces a multi-burst flower pat-
tern with a crackling torrent of sound.

"Beautiful," his mother says, and they watch the finale together and Kent pretends she is his nanny—
someone who cares for him and tends to him. This way,
Noe can become something else. They can start a new
path, a new love together.

Kent and his mother watch the fronds of light and
listen to the deafening squeals like jets right over their
heads. It's as if they're being bombed, and Kent smiles.
It's his grandfather up there in the sky flying his jet
over their heads. It's his grandfather finally at peace because he is above the island, alone, surrounded by steel
and controls. He apologizes to Gramps for using his
apology mission for the wrong reasons. He wasn't doing
it for him, but for Noe. Kent wishes he were up there
with his grandfather because being around his parents
in a place filled with beauty and flowers and sharp per-
fumes has to be the loneliest place in the world. His
heart begins to move toward his legs. The soldiers point
pistols at the tears in his eyes and they say to the tears:
"Don't move."

"Your father is too much," his mother says.

Kent follows her gaze and sees his father dancing toward Noe.

"Stop him," Kent tells his mother.

"She loves it," his mom says, clapping.

Another squeal from Operation Retribution and Kent takes it as a sign to kick some ass. He could Donkey Kick his father right here on the dance floor. Kent goes onto the dance floor, steps behind Noe, and she turns to face him. She is smiling. She seems terribly happy.

"I'm sorry," he says to her.

"It's what I do," she says.

"I'm sorry for tonight and for misbehaving in general and for the fact that you've had to spend so much time with me."

"It's been fine," she says. "You're a good kid. Relatively."

"I've changed, though, haven't I? The mission went well tonight? I'm responsible now."

Noe laughs. "It was fun," she says, "but it was just another one of your antics and I was following along as usual, making sure you didn't go too far."

"But you like our life together, right? You don't want it to end."

She places her hands on his hips. "Here. You wanted to dance, so dance. Do it the ladies' way. Go in figure eights. Hit your hips against my fingers, then the heel of my hand."

Kent does as he's told. He tries to ignore her touch and the scent of her hands. He tries not to imagine himself rubbing lotion into her elbows. He looks over her shoulder and his dad winks at him.

"What were you talking about with my dad?" Kent asks. "Did he proposition you? Threaten you? Did he try to fondle you? He does that, you know."

"I'm moving back in with him, Kent," Noe says.

"No way," Kent says. "I'm not going back there."

"You're right. You're not. I'm moving in. He needs help around the house. He misses me, I guess. Who knows what will happen?" She smiles. "You know me— enterprising and practical. I have to think about what's best for me."

"He's not what's best for you. I'm what's best for you." Kent doesn't want to see her on one of his father's tapes rocking back and forth, her face seemingly unoccupied. "He'll rape you," he says.

"Kent," Noe says. "That's an awful thing to say. Your father and I are friends. I don't want to work forever."

"My turn," Kent's father says. He puts his hands on Noe's hips then spins her around. She stumbles into him, laughs, and resumes dancing. They look as though they belong together, as if they've danced together before. Kent looks at Noe's tan legs, imagines one of them draped over his father's shoulder. The image seems right, familiar. The image, he realizes, is a memory.

"You perv," Kent says.

Noe looks over her shoulder at him. "Kent. Be nice."

"Why are you sticking up for him?" Kent asks. He can't believe what is happening. "You're sick," he says.

"You're a slut. You're a money-hungry slut." He can smell gunpowder, the scent of celebration and war. Noe turns to face him. She shakes her head and her tendrils swing. "Poor boy," she says, and he nods. She lifts her arms and he slides into them and she holds him around the neck.

"That's better," he says.

"Good," she says, and he begins to sway in her arms and they dance rocking from foot to foot. She wraps one of her arms around his waist. He begins to dance the way she has taught him, but he does it against her dress. His hips knock into her hipbones. He can feel her body against his dick. The drums are so loud and the DJ is playing rock music along with the Tahitian music. Kent can't help himself. He feels so good.

"You're the sick one," she whispers, "and don't ever speak to me that way again. I'm not yours." She bites his ear and he bends forward, immediately recognizing what is happening. He is being given the Secret Clutch, one of his grandfather's fighting moves. *To those around you, it will look like a fond embrace.* She holds him steady and then he feels her hand seizing his testicles. He cries into her shoulder and she whispers, "You need to grow up, Kent. You need to learn to live without me." She squeezes harder. "And don't rub up against me. I raised you. I loved you."

"Let go," Kent gasps.

"I'm going to let go," Noe whispers. "I'm going to leave you just as everyone else has and you're going to deal with it the best you can. You're going to make Gramps proud. You're going to grow up and be a man, and not a man like these fools around you, and I'm going to do what I have to do, too," and with that she lets go and Kent falls to the ground. He can hear people gasp above him. He can hear Noe telling everyone to give him some air.

"Get up," the soldiers say. "You're going to be left behind. Get off the dance floor. It's going to blow. It's rigged," they chant. "It's rigged." They look at him as if they've lost one of their own. He can't move and the voices fade and he looks up and sees his dad presiding over him as if he's dead.

Kent rolls onto his side then gets up. "Bit of a fainting spell," he says. "Tad too much to drink." Everyone laughs and claps. Kent waves off any help. He looks at Noe, then at his father, and he walks alone toward the handle of the yard. He tries to get a good breath.

"You okay?" It's Brandy, his friend Brandy.

"I want to be," he says.

She puts a hand on his back.

"I fainted," he says. "And now I might barf. And I need to move on."

"Yes," she says. "You fainted. That was whack."

He holds her hand because he's not quite steady. He looks at the boundary of the island, imagines it swelling and one day bursting at its rock seams. He looks back at the dance floor, at history, at the people who don't want him, at the things he and Brandy will supposedly inherit. The soldiers have gone. "Whack," he says. And he repeats this until the familiar word becomes something else entirely, as if through repetition something new can be born. Whack, whack, whack, whack, whack, whack, whack. Brandy tells him he sounds like a duck. Or a machete cutting a path.

Ancient Weapons

Earlier today, Max's wife had called from California asking him to send the ancient weapons. Max had said, "Sure. Fine," though he had no intention of sending her anything. He believed there were certain privileges the deserted should have—the friends, the house, the animals—and certain obligations they should be pardoned from—being cordial and mature, forwarding messages, and dispatching the discarded or forgotten. He wouldn't send the ancient weapons, actual Hawaiian artifacts, bludgeons, and javelins that, as Lily said, she had rightfully acquired, or, as Max said, she had silently auctioned using his credit card.

Her manner of delivering the request—entitled, snippety, toy-dog-like, had inspired Max to do time on the punching bag, a new purchase he had made along with two sets of gloves in case his daughter ever felt like hitting something. He'd bought her a pair hoping she would. Before he bought the Everlast he imagined it rocking about wildly, yet whenever he placed a punch, the sack barely moved. His knuckles and wrists were now achy, as well as his right foot, which he had used to kick the bag. If he had known the thing was going to be so unyielding, he wouldn't have bought it. He could have just punched and kicked the refrigerator.

After having been beaten by a bag, Max took his time showering and for the first time used his wife's deep conditioner she had left behind. The directions recommended it sit atop his head for five minutes. The conditioner was probably more than a year old. He had never gotten around to throwing it out and he occasionally liked to smell it. He stood in the shower and looked at his watch. He couldn't remember the last time he had just stood in a shower without doing some kind of work—lathering, scrubbing, rinsing. His wife, Lily, could stand in a shower and not do anything. She could even take baths. That whore, Max thought, and then covered his mouth even though he didn't say it aloud. Lily should have taken Mele. Or let her visit at least. A girl should be with her mother. Her mother: if he had known the thing was going to be so unyielding he wouldn't have married it. After his shower, Max shaved and nicked himself on purpose.

Through the bathroom door he could hear his daughter yelling his name. "Don't shout," he shouted, then opened the door and looked down the hall, where he saw her glowering face jutting from the doorway of her room.

"Someone's knocking on the door," she said.

Everything she said sounded ominous, even phrases such as, "Do you want an apple?" She scared the hell out of him.

"Well, can you get it? I'm bleeding," he said, pointing to the cut. He noticed this made Mele smile. "Those are our guests, remember?"

"No," she said, sulking her way to the front door.

Max saw that she clearly had remembered—she was dressed in a kimono and the guests' kimonos hung over her arm. Also, earlier he had seen her talking to Franny Kubota, the woman who cooked and served for Sukiyaki Night, an annual dinner Max and Lily hosted for their adjacent neighbors. For some reason, Mele's dishonesty pleased him. He shook his head and said her name twice: Mele Mele.

She was sixteen and her name was becoming more and more inappropriate. It translated into "song," but his daughter was hardly that. She was a deflated tire— once full and moving, now punctured and puddled under a steely weight. Max wondered what the Hawaiian word was for "deflated tire." She was always alone, either in her room or in the hammock under the banyan tree. Always reading books about crazy women. Sometimes Max would leaf through her novels while she was away. Women drowning, women in hospital wards, women going mad looking at yellow wallpaper—these were the plots of her books. Max was convinced that she thought he had driven her mother away, that Mele considered Lily to be some kind of feminist heroine, abandoning marriage and children. This made Max want to nick himself again.

Lily was hardly a heroine. She fell in love with an activist from the Office of Hawaiian Affairs, an activist/yoga instructor who had bought a "healing studio" in Mill Valley. Kind of hard to be a Hawaiian activist in Marin, ya think? This, one of the many comebacks he was amassing. One of the many retorts he said to his reflection in the bathroom mirror.

Max got dressed then peered down the other end of the hallway. He saw Mele greeting Stella and George Denby, the next-door neighbors who always drove because it was likely to rain in Maunawili and Stella feared getting her hair wet. He watched her ask the Denbys if she could get them anything to drink and he experienced a small explosion of guilt. She really was a good kid; it was just getting so hard to love her. She wouldn't talk to him—just Hi's and 'Bye's and I'm Fine's. She didn't rebel as Max expected her to—she didn't run off with boys from public schools or wear short skirts, exposed thongs, or steel-toed boots, or whatever girls did to upset their fathers, but instead she treated Max as if he were a stranger; not an alluring stranger, but the kind who lured you into danger with Jawbreakers or Pez. Maybe she needed to be provoked,

Max thought. Challenged. Maybe he would start tonight. Something needed to change. His other neighbor and friend, Judge Resner, had died last week, his ashes now scattered at the base of Olomana, the mountain Max woke to every morning. The death seemed to amplify Max's urgency to reconnect with Mele. Something between them needed to be crushed, and then revived.

Before continuing into the main room, Max stopped and prepared himself. He put on his kimono. This would be the first Sukiyaki Night without the Judge (and Lily). Tonight was to be more of a business meeting than a party. Beatrice Resner had asked Max and the Denbys to name the park her husband had made at the bottom of their property. Tonight they'd decide on a name.

Max walked down the narrow hallway with its dim, flickering light. He loved this part of his home—the narrow hall—not for the hall itself but for the effect its narrowness had upon the room it led into—an open space, which served as the living room and the dining room. Whenever he reached this room, he felt as if he had rediscovered something, an old memory or money in a pocket. He walked toward the hushed voices. The Denbys were negotiating their drinks and their tempura, nibbling on the golden arcs of shrimp and vegetables, their kimonos layered over their normal outfits. Max smiled; he loved the familiarity, the tradition of this somewhat kitschy theme party, but then he remembered that Joe Resner was dead and put on a face he thought looked long and distraught.

"Mr. Max Glum!" George said. "Why so glum? I'll rob a bank to get you to smile. How about it?"

Max pretended to be amused and he was, a little. He liked that George yelled everything. George shook his hand until he realized that shaking hands wouldn't do and so embraced Max in a rough and quick clutch. Stella hugged and pecked the air around him. The Denbys were in their late eighties. Stella was aware of this but George was not.

"Hello, everyone," Max said. "Well," he said. "Well, well, well. Where's Beatrice?"

"She thought we'd be more comfortable choosing a name without her," Stella said.

"Yes," Max said. "That makes sense. And . . ." He noticed a man standing off to the side, flipping through a photo album. The Judge's yardman? He gestured to the man.

"Yes," Stella said, lowering her voice, her eyes blinking with annoyance, "that's Beatrice's yard helper."

"Jeffery," the man said, looking up from the album, his eyes glassy, face dark and weathered.

"Hey. Long time no see," Max said, reverting to pidgin English. Mele snorted out a crude laugh.

"I never knew this was one party for deviants," Jeffery said.

"What's that?" Max asked.

Jeffery gestured to his kimono hanging over his jeans.

He fluttered the drooping arms of the dress and batted his eyelashes.

"Oh," Max said. "Ha ha. Yes. Well."

Mele laughed again. He used her laughter as an opportunity. He joined her—ha ha!—put his arm casually around her, which she skillfully turned into a kind of dance move, turning into him then revolving out and away. During this spin Max caught a whiff of her hair. She, too, had used his wife's conditioner.

"Why don't we go outside?" Stella said.

Max moved with his guests silently past the screen doors and into the darkness.

He stood next to Mele. Her hair was situated in an elegant loose knot atop her head. Her hair was now a source of pride for Max. The texture of it and its golden brown color was something she had in common with him. It was something Lily did not have. Lily's hair was black and kinked and, according to the biology books, should have won the genetic fight. Max thought it was magical that his recessive gene survived. Her face looked radiant and clean, apparently without makeup, yet Max knew it was there somewhere—a trick her mother had mastered, mixing and blending until her face seemed to blossom from somewhere earthy and nutritious. Mele's face was in bloom, a kind of night-light, budding from her thin body. Max almost looked away, stung by her calm. Her pleased expression, the slight upswing of her lips, the way she seemed to be listening to some internal music; he sensed all of it was forged and difficult to maintain. He wanted to tell her it was okay to drop the act. Max considered shaking her until she cried out, until she was completely messy, ugly, her hair and makeup in full disarray. Instead he reached out and squeezed the bun atop her head. He had never seen a person react so quickly—his hand was immediately swatted away.

"Don't," she said. "It's hard to arrange." She stared into the distance and then mumbled, "Thief."

"What?" he asked. "What did you say?" Mele wouldn't answer.

"Were you the guy who came over that time for one pumalo?" Jeffery asked.

"Yes," Max said, turning to Jeffery. "Such a robust fruit." He regretted his description immediately, but was distracted. Did she just call him a thief?

"Yeah," Jeffery said. "Big fruit."

Max wondered if Jeffery was his real name. He was Mexican or Filipino. Or Hawaiian and Chinese. Something. He'd be willing to bet his real name was Pablo or Fernando or Carlos. "So the park is finally finished," Max said, fishing for why this man was in his home.

Jeffery tugged on his kimono, which was parting like a curtain. "Yeah," he said. "All finished. That's why Judge's wife told me come over here and help you guys with one name."

"Yes, of course," Max said. "That makes sense. I'm sure Joe is very proud of your work." Max let the silent night lend some gravity to his statement and then turned to see what the others were up to.

"He was," Jeffery said.

"Pardon?"

"He was proud. But not now. He's dead, that's why. Judge always said, when you dead, you no can see."

Max wasn't sure how to respond, but Jeffery continued.

"Judge liked it that way. No worries that way."

Max nodded. He wished he could enjoy that theory but he preferred the idea of heaven—a place where he could watch the world age. Perhaps see his wife again. Break her halo or kick her in the ass when no one was looking.

Jeffery sighed. "I can't think of nothing. A name for the park."

"I'm sure we'll think of something," Max said, then retreated to the view. The sight of Mount Olomana was startling tonight.

"Look at that moon," Stella said. "Right at Olomana's peak."

"Like a head on a woman wearing a hoop skirt," George said. "A woman without a torso."

Max looked at Mele. "Nice, isn't it? The moon."

"I guess," she said, staring at the ground, and then she lifted her leg and brought her foot back down on a huge cockroach. She dragged her slipper across the tile and Max could see a gelatinous trail of white guts. Wow, he thought, and suddenly he longed for her to be mean to him, remembering an incident about a week after Lily had left. He had tucked her in, kissed her on the lips as he'd always done.

"You're disgusting," she said, a remark that made him feel just that.

"So are you," he said.

For a moment they were so angry at each other, so sickened by the situation forced upon them that it formed this frayed yet resilient thread between them. And they laughed. They laughed! Max went to bed that night and cried.

But the thread quickly snapped. Mele was just okay with it all, or pretended to be, relishing the gloom like the characters in her books. Max often crept to her closed door and listened to find out if *she* cried at night, if something broke when she was alone. Caught you! he would say, but he only heard the rustling of books and the occasional sneeze. Max would tiptoe away thinking he was the cause of her sneezing, that perhaps she was allergic to him.

"The moon's floating away from its body," George said, raising his drink to the sky.

Max looked up and watched the mountain lose its head.

Max smiled at the recognition of all the table settings: the porcelain plates with blue-blossom motifs, the onyx bowls with gold, haphazard lines; the lacquered chopsticks resting on small wooden fish, porcelain leaves which held eggs, sake glasses, sterling goblets for water (not very Japanese, Lily always said), five stout cups for tea, and the bamboo place mats. The candles were doing their thing: burning, melting, creating atmosphere. The centerpiece was a woolly-lip fern in a fishbowl glass. It was placed at the head of the table where he always had Joe sit. The sea-green fronds hung over the bluish glass. Max went to the end of the table, touched the leaves of the plant, and felt acutely aware of those absent.

Franny Kubota came from the swinging kitchen door with a wood tray. She waved quickly at Max and he grinned, for some reason so ecstatic by her presence, her familiar face, white dress, that sad small hump rounding her shoulders. She completed the evening—the Japanese cook—lent it more . . . *stuff.*

Max asked Jeffery to sit to his left, where Beatrice would have been seated. Mele sat to Max's right. He put his arm around the back of her chair. She scooted herself in and his arm dropped. He put his hand on her back. What could she possibly do? What she did was wait it out like a storm, head tilted down as if praying for it to advance. Max removed his hand—that frightening squall—routed it in an easterly direction to his silverware.

First there was miso soup and namasu, and then the main course. When Franny served Max a bowl of white rice and sukiyaki, he quickly cracked his egg into the bowl then stirred the hot noodles, meat, and vegetables so the egg could cook. He stirred until the goop of the egg had transformed into strings. He watched his daughter place her napkin onto her lap, pleased. He watched her take a shot of sake, displeased.

"That-a girl," George said. He sat across from her.

"Look at you, Mele. Just beautiful! You look just like your mother." After he finished his sentence George cringed. Had Stella kicked him under the table?

"Thank you," Mele said.

"I mean you look just like a woman all grown up," George said.

"That's good to know," Mele said, and smiled kindly. She leaned forward to ask Jeffery if he liked sukiyaki.

"Not as good as black dog," Jeffery said, and then laughed. "Just joke."

"Speaking of animals," George said. "The old over-weight penguin at Sea Life Park died yesterday! Poor boy. Wasn't he a riot? The penguin. Penguin," he shouted.

"Speaking of Sea Life Park," Stella said. "Have you seen the eyesore across the street from it? Tents, banners, flags flapping everywhere. And rubbish! Beer cans on the side of the road, which happens to be our adopted highway. Do you ever drive that way, Max?"

"Rarely," Max lied. It was the last thing he wanted to talk about. Stella was referring to the Hawaiians who had set up camp in Waimanalo. They were activists for a separate state. Let them have their separate state, Max thought. He wondered if he could join them.

"I go that way," Mele said.

"Well, what do you think, dear?" Stella asked.

"I'm not sure. What do you think?"

He wondered if she was like her mother in this way. Lily liked to turn the conversation over, testing to see if the person was worth her contention.

"I think it's ridiculous," Stella said. "Do they want to go back to the old ways? The old ways were like feudal Europe."

"If you stepped in the queen's shadow you got your head cut off," George said. "And she was a pretty hefty queen. Hard to miss."

"It's just silly to want to go back," Stella said. "Why would anyone want to go back? Violent rulers, inane laws, no freedom, caste systems, slavery, my God."

"That's not how it was during annexation," Mele said.

"There's no turning back," George said. "Same reason we can't get a divorce. We're in it for the long run."

"I don't see what those people are fighting for," Stella said.

"They're fighting for land," Mele said. "Of course they don't want to go back to the caste systems."

"Well, you can't pick and choose," Stella said.

"Yes, you can," Mele said. "That's the whole point. And we don't know what it was really like before the monarchy. My mother said that it's so hard to separate history from myth when it comes to Hawaiian history."

"Well, their savage ways were not a myth," Stella said.

"Neither are yours," Mele said. "I mean, Europeans."

Max quickly swallowed his food. "When did your mom say this? When did you talk to her?"

Mele took a sip of water, an infuriatingly long sip. She turned to Max. "While you were in the shower. She wants her weapons back."

"What's with the weapons? Why is she so desperate to have them all of a sudden?"

"Duane wanted to see them. He thinks it's incredible she has them. He wants to take them to an antiques show."

"Duane," Max said. "I see." Max looked up, tried to gauge whether or not the Denbys were paying attention. George was attempting to pinch Stella's hand with his chopsticks and she was attempting not to smile.

"What's all this about weapons?" Stella asked.

"Nothing," Max said, perhaps a bit rudely.

"What should we name the park?" Jeffery asked.

The dinner party turned to Jeffery as if a shy child had suddenly spoken.

"Yes, I suppose we should get started on that," Stella said, swiping the corners of her mouth with a finger. "One idea that I thought of while I was at my Adventures Club meeting was calling it the Isabella Bird, after the lady travel writer from Yorkshire who called our volcanoes 'the mysterious furnaces of the Apocalypse.'"

Max tried to think of a way to tell Stella that was the dumbest idea he'd ever heard. "Or perhaps something a bit more relevant to Joe's life," he said.

"Whistle," Jeffery said. "Whistle Park. Judge always whistling, that's why. Not good, though. Off-key. Too much air. Like this." Jeffery blew air through his lips, letting one note of music slide into his breath.

George joined in, whistling a low flat pitch. "Yes!" George said.

"That's good, Jeffery," Max said. "That's the idea.

Why not continue this way—throw out ideas, or names relevant to Joe's life?"

Stella stabbed a mushroom with her chopstick. Max tried to think of something good. When he was twenty-four he had clerked for Joe and since then they had become friends, talking shop, trading stories. It was Joe who had told him about the house he now owns, and at the time it had made him feel like the teacher's pet.

Max concentrated on the sweet meat, the snap of a snap pea, the crack of a water chestnut. He sipped his sake, felt the heat of the rice wine warm his face and throat. He tried to think of a name, the best name, one that would supersede any other and ring the others' hearts with its rightness, one that would landmark his sentiments and immortalize someone he loved. His lack of ideas made him feel disloyal somehow, anxious, as well—he felt it was right there—the perfect word that would make Mele nod in recognition of her father's ability to find resolution and accord. He wanted to show her he could be counted on. As a baby she used to grip a thatch of his hair as if her life depended on it. Perhaps he wanted her to do a version of this again, or perhaps it was he who needed a thatch to hold on to. He looked at her bun, a knob atop her head, a perfect globe to cushion his palm. He could not think of a name.

So, what do we have so far?" Stella asked. "We have Isabella Bird, Olomana, the Scales, Objection . . ."

"That's got my vote," George said.

". . . Black Robe, and Whittling." Stella took an exaggerated breath of air.

"Whistling," Mele said. "Not Whittling, and you forgot the name I suggested: Pahoa Park."

"Oh yes," Stella said. "That pretty Hawaiian name."

Dessert was appearing in droves. Brownies, fortune cookies, coffee with spoons covered in hardened chocolate.

"What's my fortune this year?" George cracked his cookie like an egg on the edge of his dessert dish.

"No fortunes this year," Mele said. "Dad forgot."

Every previous year, Lily had ordered empty fortune cookies from a bakery, typed the fortunes, and then slipped them into the mouth of the cookie. Last year he received the appropriate caution: *Don't listen to anyone who stuffs paper into cookies.*

"Sorry," Max said. "I'm becoming forgetful and useless. Please, somebody push me off a cliff." Stella laughed, though he was being sincere.

"Like King Kamehameha!" George said.

"I wonder what possessed them to have a war on the edge of a cliff," Stella said. "Or was that just a myth, Mele?"

Mele finished chewing then patted her mouth with her napkin. "My mother and me, we're both Hawaiian. Did you know that, Mrs. Denby?"

"Yes, I did, dear. You're so lucky."

Now Mele was pulling the Hawaiian card. Lily used to do the same thing. The woman card. The minority card.

"She's a teaspoon Hawaiian," Max announced, patting Mele on the head. "A stitch. A smidgen. A shot glass full." Max took a shot of sake to illustrate his analogy. He looked at Jeffery, nudged him for a laugh. Jeffery shook his head.

"It was your mother who first told me about all the illogical hoopla the separatists were creating," Stella said. "'Much ado about Oahu,' she said."

Max smiled and then stopped as he realized he was getting such joy out of seeing his child defeated, and perhaps disillusioned. He realized with her here, here with her fresh face and clever eyes and soft arrogant voice, he was having trouble differentiating between her and a woman long gone. Yet Lily wouldn't have allowed the conversation to rest there. She had to have the final utterance, which always possessed a maddening resonance. A winner of all arguments, even the little ones, even the subtle ones; she commanded them, steered them right into her lap. Yet this was his child. This was Mele, his heartbreaking song of a daughter.

"My mother often changed her opinions to suit her company," Mele said. "She gauged what people would and would not understand. But to answer your question, it wasn't a myth. King Kamehameha fought on many mountain ranges. He was a fearless warrior. It was the way battles were fought."

Stella smiled.

Max was wrong. Lily and Mele were exactly alike. But Mele was stronger. She spoke in such a carefree way, a sort of take-it-or-leave-it tactic so you couldn't discard her.

"Cheers to King Kamehameha!" George said, raising his sake cup. "Ruler of the islands. Lord of the dance!"

"Stop drinking, George. You're not good at that anymore."

"Mele, did you know *I* was a warrior? I was in Vietnam," George said.

"He was an engineer, dear. He built bridges," Stella said.

"Still, I was in danger," George said.

"Joe did a good job," Jeffery said. "He helped me do everything in the yard."

Max was uncomfortable with the silence that followed and with Jeffery's apparent sadness. He was relieved by the noise Franny was making, filling the water glasses and clearing dessert plates.

"You were one of his best friends," Mele said. "You probably knew him better than anyone here."

Jeffery looked at his lap and nodded.

"Well," Stella said softly. "A tad disproportionate."

But Mele was right. An itch of envy filled Max's chest; a familiar tickle that had appeared when Lily was still at home. Lily and Mele had been inseparable, they even argued up close, never across rooms, and while Max was happy for this, he also knew it was a relationship that he couldn't enter. Joe and Jeffery had worked side by side for years, probably not talking much, but getting things done, clearing things out. Visible results.

Theirs was a closeness comprised of sweat and heart. With Lily gone, he assumed Mele would look to him to work with, to team up with; in fact he expected it as the one benefit. They didn't have to talk. Max didn't even need that much. He just wanted something to happen between them—something to show for all of this.

"I was thinking—Fortune Park," Jeffery said. "Just tonight I got that idea. From dessert."

"Fortune Park is a good name," Max said. He felt a feeling of rightness. A certain briskness seemed to spike the warm air with sadness and lucidity.

"I like that, Jeffery," Mele said. "We'll have fortunes after all."

"Or the Scales," Stella said. "He *was* a judge, after all. He told me he loved collecting those pictures of old courthouses. The Scales, the Scales." Stella mouthed this again and again, testing it out.

"Or, perhaps, Samuel Adams Park," George said. "He loved that beer. He used to come over and he would drink two Samuel Adams beers and no more than two and he'd sit with me until I had my five or so. It's a real quality ale."

"I'm not sure Joe would be so keen. . . . Think, everyone," Stella said. "Think of some pretty word."

"What does Pahoa mean?" Jeffery asked.

"Wooden dagger," Mele said.

"What?" Stella asked, a speck of brownie on her chin. "Why in the world would we name the park Wooden Dagger?"

"Because it's also a name for yard tools," Mele said, "used to clear and cut. And land is territory that's fought for. In his own way, Joe fought for the land he lived on. He grew up on a farm in Kansas and worked hard to go to college and Boalt, and then make a name for himself here, but I like Fortune Park anyway."

Max smiled, surprised by his daughter, her thoroughness and passion, but then he was reminded of the weapons and guessed that her mother had suggested the name on the phone earlier today. It explained how she knew so much about Joe. He was annoyed that Lily had managed to find her way to the table, and even possibly choose the name of the park.

"Well, we'll think of something," Stella said.

"Fortune Park," Mele said. "We've already thought of something."

"Perhaps we should sleep on it," Stella said.

"We've already decided," Mele said louder, her voice slightly trembling. "Jeffery has the right to name the park and it's a good name. We all think so. He helped to actually make the park. It's his. It's his park." She knocked her sake cup against the wood table as if hammering a gavel.

Jesus, Max thought; it had been a while since he'd seen her excited about something. He didn't know what to say. He looked at Stella, expecting her to be replaced by a gelatinous trail, like the one that followed the cockroach.

"No worries," Jeffery said. "Just a name."

Like a cockroach, Stella survived. She put an end to the conversation. "Oh, look," she said. "It's going to rain. I knew it."

Max and everyone else followed her gaze. Clouds had screened the moon and a ghostly gray of rain wavered like a flock of birds along the ridges of the Ko'olaus.

Max had let Franny go early, wanting to clean up for himself. As he finished wiping the counters he heard noises that sounded like sobbing. He hesitated, hopeful.

"Mele?" he called from the kitchen before entering the living room.

Mele was wrapped in an afghan watching the television. It was the television sobbing, not his daughter. He sat on the couch beside her.

"That was interesting tonight," he said.

"Right," she said. "Interesting."

"Sort of combative," he said. "Sorry about Mrs. Denby. She can be a bit stuffy and irritating."

She looked at him, head tilted, one eyebrow raised. Max looked at this eyebrow. It was very nicely shaped.

"I don't think you should be the one to apologize," she said.

"What do you mean?"

"You can be a bit irritating yourself. You could have said you wanted Fortune Park, too. It's Jeffery's park."

"It's not his park. He's an employee."

"See what I mean?" she said. "You're just like her.

Mrs. Brownie Face." She got up from the couch and turned off the television. Max could see she had gathered her mother's weapons. They were next to the sofa, glinting from a brown box—the shark's-teeth knife, the stone battleaxe, the pahoa, club, spear, and the pièce de résistance, the mahiole: feathered war helmet. He stared at the box.

"Mom said you probably wouldn't send them, so I will."

"She left them," Max said. "Why would I send them? She left the things she didn't want, remember?"

"It doesn't matter," she said. "They're hers. Someone like you doesn't deserve them."

"Duane wanted them. You even said so. It's not as if she cares about them."

"Of course she cares. They're anthropology. They're history—our history."

"Did she ask you to come, too? Or just the weapons?"

"I'm going to bed," Mele said.

It was all he'd get from his daughter, who cautiously and cowardly hid behind indifference, protecting a woman who manipulated her, who left her. "Chicken," he said.

"What?"

"Never mind," he said, imitating her soft voice.

"You can be so odd." She took the blanket off from around her shoulders, folded it, and placed it on the arm of the couch. She was wearing her white silk pajamas and Max noticed her high breasts bumped up against the silk. They were her mother's breasts, small and perfect. They sickened him.

"That wasn't your idea—Pahoa. It was hers, wasn't it?"

"So?" she said. She had her back to him.

"So, be yourself. Come up with your own ideas. Stop trying to be like her."

She looked back at him quizzically, as if he were some kind of notable artifact; she waited him out, and again her patience overcame him and altered his course. "I'm sorry," he said. "I'm just trying to talk. I'm hurt. I miss her. I hate her. I'm sorry."

"I'm going to resemble her," she said. "I can't help it. So go ahead and hate me."

"I don't hate you," Max said.

"Well, I hate you," she said.

"What did I do wrong, Mele? I didn't leave you. What can I do for you?"

The rain outside seemed to be coming in sets—gushing then receding, gushing then receding. The sound saddened him. He thought that when she called him a thief she had been referring to the weapons but now he wondered if she was referring to herself, if she believed he had stolen her somehow. He looked at her, her arms crossed against her chest, and he felt like a thief—that she was someone who didn't belong to him. He wondered if she thought he belonged to her. It seemed critical to him just then that she did believe this, that she understood that Max was hers.

"Wait here," he said. He went to the basement,

headed for the punching bag. He thought of the party tonight—the naming of the park and what that meant, really. They were all declaring their turf in the Judge's heart, fighting for a place in his life. No one had ever done that for Max. No one had fought to stake their claim of him. But Max realized he had never done it either. He certainly hadn't fought for Lily. He just let her go and she went. He grabbed the gloves and went back to the living room.

Mele was in the same place as he left her. Still standing and gazing at something—the air, the future, the wallpaper, who knew? Max stood in front of her. He threw a pair of gloves at her and they hit her chest and dropped to the floor. She stared at the gloves. Max put his gloves on and pounded his fists together and hopped around. He hopped around his daughter.

"Put 'em on," he said. "Go on."

Mele slipped them on gracefully as if they were kid gloves. She held out her hands and pondered them.

"All right," Max said. "Let's go." He made the sound of a bell. "Ding ding."

Mele didn't move. Max held his gloved hands in front of him. They looked like the bulbous heads of animals peeking out of their burrows.

"Well, go, then," Mele said. "If you want to hit me, then hit me." She opened her arms as if she wanted a hug. Like a starting bell or a green flag, the white blanket fell from the couch and pooled on the floor next to the box of weapons.

Max jumped in place and took some warm-up swings. He could still hear the rain falling on Olomana, the park and the gray ashes.

"Go on," Mele said. "Ding ding."

Max jabbed at the air and bounced from foot to foot. He was panting and sweating and felt absurd and elderly. He stopped bounding about, bent over, and tried to catch his breath. He stayed there for a while, stooped and weak, squeezed his eyes closed, and tried to breathe. He stood up straight and felt his eyes watering. He covered his face with his ridiculous gloves. "I'm sorry, Mele. I don't know what I'm doing. I'm trying to fight for you. I want you to fight for me. I'm just so sad. I'm so——"

"Just shut up," Mele said.

Max moved his hands away from his eyes only to see Mele wearing the war helmet, a headdresslike creation cradling her face and rising like a question mark above her head. He laughed. "Mele," he said, looking at her in her nightgown and war helmet and boxing gloves. She was the epitome of confusion, and she seemed to wear it well.

He waited for her to smile but instead she pulled her arm back, her glove like an arrow aimed at his heart, her stance secure and grounded. At first he was angry because she was so humorless, so unnecessarily hostile. Why couldn't she just laugh with him and be done with it? In the moment before contact, however, Max saw something in Mele besides pure rage. Something kind. Something resilient. Something that resembled that old frayed thread. He wished there was a name for what he felt, or a name for the feeling that comes after a hard punch: the cold blow, the sharp sting, the powerful, terrible ache, and then the startling warmth.

His daughter's fist moved toward his face. This was the moment; this was the way their battle would be resolved, the way they would come to rightfully own one another. Some people fought on cliffs, others in living rooms, and he felt this was as important a battle as any.

Max stood still. He believed that the incoming hit would be enough to knock him down or, more realistically, knock him back. She would move him. He would move for her. She would see the results of her punch.

Location Scouts

Letta is in the backseat of my car, sulking like a child. If she were my child I'd put her on time-out. I'd put liquid soap in her mouth and tell her to gargle while I ranted about sacrifices and respect. I'd put my hand over my head and say that I had it up to here, but she is not my child. She's my neighbor's daughter, seventeen years old. Her family moved in a year ago. Lately, on Sundays it's her routine to stand by my car and demand to go wherever I'm going. On Sundays this is always to an apartment-showing. I take her to one of my listings, let her hand out fact sheets and tell her not to speak to anyone. She is usually well behaved. She roams around the apartment, looking through drawers and cupboards. She looks at people's photographs. She lounges on patio chairs on the terraces that overlook Waikiki and Diamond Head. All of my listings have oceanfront lanais; the Pacific is the backyard. They are all gorgeous. The fact sheets say, "Spectacular Views," "Exclusive Property," and "Dream Location." My listings are in buildings called Diamond Sands and Sans Souci; in French this means "without care."

Today came as a surprise to Letta because I didn't take her to an apartment. I took her to a wake, a baby's wake in Waianae. We have just left the wake and are driving home. I drive carefully at night.

I look at her in the rearview mirror. Headlights of a passing car on the other side of the highway momentarily light her face. There's a muscle rising from her chest, climbing her neck like a weed. Her hair is in pigtails. She's that kind of girl—the kind that wears pigtails, sucks on Blow Pops, wears short shorts that say JUICY on the butt. She's a total slut, I bet. I don't know why she hangs around me. We don't get along. If I were her age I'd sneak up to her while she was asleep, and with sharp scissors I'd snip away one of her tails of hair, but I'm not her age; I'm thirty-five, and so I remind myself to be nice to her because she's a young girl with a sick mother and could probably use some female guidance. Her mother lives with a nurse in a studio behind their main house. As far as I know she rarely enters the main house. Letta's father is a college basketball coach. He's always surrounded by boys who in groups look strong and threatening, but when alone look cumbersome and unfit for this world. The college is at the bottom of my hill.

I see the boys walking around in their tank tops. I see the girls looking at the boys in their tank tops.

Letta hasn't spoken to me since we left the wake. "Cat got your tongue?" I ask. "Giraffe got your neck?"

"That's so lame," she says, but I see a twitch of amusement move across her mouth.

Then we are silent once again, in the eye of a storm. She's upset, but her irritation is unearned. By going to the wake, I expected to teach her a lesson, which was don't demand to be taken somewhere unless you know where somewhere is. My lesson backfired. She loved the wake. She wasn't ready to leave. She claimed she was having a ball.

"You can't have a ball at a wake," I said as we left, walking down the driveway of crushed shells.

"I can have a ball anywhere," she said. "And it wasn't a wake. You missed the whole point."

Until tonight I have never been to Waianae even though I've lived on Oahu my entire life. I'm the Gold Coast specialist; selling apartments all along that particular stretch of south shore. Waianae isn't part of that stretch. It's kind of a scary place. Locals only. That sort of thing. Ronnie Kealana, a realtor whose desk is next to mine; his son died. Ronnie was prepared for it. The baby died two days ago. He was six months old.

I was prepared for my baby dying, as well. In fact, I scheduled it. I had an abortion two and a half years ago, though they didn't call it an abortion. They called it a D&C and that's what I write down now if a medical form asks if I've had any operations. It sounds much better. I was three months along when I had it done. It was like a checkup, a pelvic exam. The usual tools—stirrups, speculum, cold metal instruments. I didn't look at anything. I felt a constant cramping and that's all. The doctor felt she had to soothe me. She told me I was doing well though I wasn't doing anything at all. She said things were looking good. She said it was all just liquid and then she said, "Oh!" and then after that, "Okay, almost done," and I always think of that "Oh!"—what it meant, what she saw, if the fetus had been bigger, more developed, than she expected.

This afternoon, Ronnie had a baby luau, traditionally a party given for a child's first birthday. All of the components of a luau were there—kalua pig, lomi lomi salmon, chicken long rice, poi, haupia, beer. His friends played music, his mother sang "Sweet Leilani." Pictures of the baby were arranged in collages on a table under the tent. I was overdressed.

Ronnie seemed to be having a good time. Saying sorry didn't seem to be appropriate, as no one there seemed to be sorry. Ronnie is a nature enthusiast and he told me about a class he was taking at Leeward Community College: Endangered Wildlife. He drank a light beer. "Did you know that Hawaii is the nation's endangered species capital?" he asked.

"No," I said.

"Hundreds of plants and animals. Almost gone. Maki. But still"—he raised his arms, gesturing to the ocean with his right hand, the mountains with his left—"there is so much life!" Then he nodded to the seated arc of men jamming on steel stringed guitars and the women dancing with their arms up in the air, heads back, thick hair brushing their full waists. "So much wild life," he said, laughing and dancing a bit.

I thought of his dead son. I almost told him that when I was a baby I had polio and nearly died, but then his wife came along and her presence somehow made me realize how stupid it would have been to share this with Ronnie. I almost didn't make it means that I made it. I didn't die. Where's the story, the lesson, in that?

He introduced me to his wife, Deb. I had met her before in the office but I could tell she didn't remember me. Her hair was the only thing about her that seemed frazzled and unprepared. I tried to think of something to say to her and Ronnie. I asked Ronnie if he ever saw an endangered animal eating an endangered plant and this made them laugh very loudly and so I laughed, too, pretending I meant to be funny.

Ronnie and Deb moved on to the food table, leaving me standing next to a very large old lady in a wheelchair whom everyone called Auntie Fat. We watched three women dance a hula about sifting through limu, which means seaweed. Auntie Fat explained to me that all Hawaiian words had double meanings and that limu also meant pubic hair.

I watched some men bring a pig out of the ground while holding their beers at the same time. I thought that if I died, I wouldn't want women dancing to songs about pubic hair, or pigs coming up and out of a hole in the ground.

So, Letta, you were having a ball, were you? Who was that guy you were talking to all night?" I ask this while yawning, check the rearview mirror, and add, "He seemed lively."

"Lively?" Letta says. "Sure, Brooke. He was lively. Indeed."

"Well, who was he?"

"Kai. Actually, a really nice guy. He's close to the Kealanas. His dad was the baby's godfather. So funny," she says from the back.

"What's so funny?"

"Kai. The guy I was talking to tonight. He snow-boards on Mauna Kea. Can you imagine? I never would have thought of doing that. I told him maybe I could join him sometime. I think I'd be good at it."

I'm sure she'd be great at it. Jumping and grabbing, or whatever those people do. I can just imagine this Kai talking loudly to his radical friends about whether he and Letta should do a synchronized flip, or if they should just light up a joint and have extreme sex.

"I did ballet when I was little. So I probably have the right skills. The balance. Should I try it?" she asks.

"Sure. Try it. You could use a hobby. Or a new friend."

"So anyway," Letta says. "Kai got to spend a lot of

time with the baby—at the hospital, and then during the last few days they brought the baby home. He said Ronnie let him hold him and the baby fell asleep on his chest and Kai petted his head with his index finger. So sad. It makes me so sad."

I wonder if it really makes her sad or if she thinks sadness looks good on her—like pink eye shadow or a nude gloss. I look at her in the rearview mirror telling me about Kai. She has a dreamy look on her face. She doesn't look sad. She looks like a rock groupie.

"Kai said that if the baby had gotten the chance to grow up, he would have taken him to play in the snow and swim in the ocean all in the same day."

"Well. Kai seems like a nice boy. Does he drive? Perhaps you could start standing by his car." I remember my age, my responsibility as the older woman. I want to be good to her, to see if it's possible. I remember that I need her on my side. I also remember her mother.

Her mother is practically paralyzed. I should have more compassion. She writes and illustrates children's books. She does adaptations, takes classic tales and gives them a local flavor. For example, *Snow White and the Seven Dwarfs* has become *Mehana and the Seven Menehunes*.

She has ALS—Lou Gehrig's disease. She wants to write and draw as much as possible before she loses control of her hands. She has lost the use of her right hand. Now she draws with her left. She is confined to a wheelchair. She has been sick for six years. This is all I know.

"So," I say. I will try to engage her. I will try to be motherly. "Where did you and Kai go? I never really saw you."

"We just drifted around, talked about the baby, listened to some music, danced, ate. Those men who sang—they made the most amazing sounds." She starts to sing something Hawaiian then stops. "Did you not have a good time tonight? Is that why you tried to spy on me?"

I turn on the radio. Useless. Nothing comes in out here. "I wasn't spying on you. I'm merely asking questions to engage you, but to answer your first question, no, I guess I didn't have that much fun tonight. We were at a baby's wake, not some sort of rave." I'm not very good at this.

"Rave?" she says. "That's passé, Brooke. You're so old." She catches my eyes in the mirror and it's as if some kind of mechanism for argument is set. "We were at a baby luau," she says.

"We were at a funeral," I say. "A baby died. How could you possibly enjoy yourself?"

"I enjoyed myself because that's what the Kealanas asked us to do. They didn't ask us to show up and cry. Tonight was a celebration of the life the baby had. Oh, and I kissed Kai goodbye. I used my tongue."

"Good for you," I say.

"Maybe that's your problem," she says. "You're so uptight. You wear panty hose, for crying out louder than ever. Maybe you just need a good screw."

"You're lovely company," I say.

"Maybe you should get it on with my dad. I see the way you look at him. All women look at him that way 'cause he's a jock with chest hair and lots of money. You probably want to do him standing up. You want to freak him on the hood of his Escalade." She laughs for a while. "You probably want to see him shoot and dunk. And dribble!" She laughs so hard I can't help but smile.

I could put an end to the laughter if I wanted to. I could tell her that I've already had sex with her father; that I've done it with him every way imaginable, that I'm dating him in secret, something we have to do since, technically, he's still married. When I ask him if I can go with him to one of his games he says, "Not yet," and I understand. He can't afford bad press right now. Just recently he received a raise that makes him the highest paid state employee, which has a lot of people in an uproar since he's just a college coach. In today's *Advertiser* more faculty expressed their outrage over his six-figure salary—$785,000 a year, to be exact. "Fowler's taking home more than our governor and we're barely getting by." "Do we want a university that is known as a basketball school with third-rate academics?" I read every article. Even when they're negative, I can't help but be proud of him and of myself—it's as if I'm in those headlines and articles, too.

I have grown fond of Letta's father. He never looks me in the eye; he never asks me questions about myself, he knows nothing of my past. He doesn't know about the car accident. There's something about this distance, this lack, that I find appealing, refreshing. I have staked new territory for myself—it isn't the nicest or most secure place, but it's property, it's my own land, it's something I can build upon.

The other week I showed him an apartment in Kapiolani Towers, a building that has one unit per floor. Two bedrooms, two baths, two parking spots. A deck that's 460 square feet. He immediately went to the lanai—everyone does—and looked down at the pool and the ocean. I stood next to him and told him he should buy it and that we should live in it together. I had opened all of the sliding doors. I wanted him to feel the difference between the open, bright apartment and the dark forest he calls home. I'm tired of living where I live—up on a hill where the air is crisp and wet. I used to love it—the trees, the altitude, the isolation—but now it's too quiet, too dark, too heavy with memories.

"What do you think?" I asked. I needed him to want the apartment, to want me in the apartment. Lately I have desired nothing more than to live in one of my listings, but I can't afford it myself. He's my way down the mountain. I came up behind him and pressed him against the black railing. We were probably both thinking that we had to wait for his wife to die.

"This is really nice," he said. We were overlooking the canoe surfers, the sunbathers, the fishing boats, the children in their floaties tumbling like laundry in the foam of the waves. Everything was so bright. Everything was sparkling.

"What would the guys think?" he asked.

The guys: his friends from high school. They have

names like "Gutter," "Sunny Boy," and "Junior." They drive big trucks and are constantly barbecuing. He's always checking himself, making sure he isn't becoming too fancy for them. I don't care, really. I like him. I need him. He's nothing like the man I love.

Letta finally stops laughing. "My dad's no good for you anyway," she says. "He likes dumb girls. And he's a bastard."

"Why do you say that?"

"I have my reasons," she says.

I look at her and this time sadness appears on her face, but it doesn't look like an accessory.

"He doesn't know what to do with me," she says. "I embarrass him. You, too. You were embarrassed to be with me tonight—I could tell."

"Well, naturally," I say, trying to get her to laugh again. "You made out with someone. At a wake."

"But you didn't know that until now. You were embarrassed of me without evidence of wrongdoing."

"Perhaps I wouldn't have been embarrassed if you wore a bra with that blouse. Or an outfit that was more somber. Wear a bra. Wear looser pants." This is my prescription to her. It's meant to be amusing.

"Are you saying I'm a slut?" she says. "You of all people. You're such a cunt."

I have nothing to say to that.

I notice that I have begun to drive incredibly fast. Blurry life whirs past us. Lush monkey pods, then dry hills, then deep ravines of flat trees and ferns. I imagine all of it verging on extinction. I imagine the two of us on the endangered list, right between Monk Seal and Nene Goose, there we are: Brooke and Letta. I shouldn't be driving this way. Accidents happen this way.

"If I'm such a ... bad person, why do you bother with me?" I ask. "Hello? Can you answer?"

"Fuck off, Brooke," she says.

She looks so angry. I wonder what I've done wrong. I take deep breaths, but I can't control myself. "You fuck off," I say. I'll never be a good mother. I'll never be a good person.

I take my exit and come to a four-way light. The light is red and when it turns green, she gets out of the car. We're not near the sidewalk—she has to cross three lanes of traffic to reach it. Cars are honking at me and I'm forced to drive, but I watch where she goes in my mirror. The cars don't frighten her—she walks through the pandemonium like a bored cat. I make a right turn and no longer see her. I realize that she would have to go into a ditch in order to get to the small shopping center, and I hope she's safe, while she's probably hoping she's in danger. I finally see her climbing over a wire fence holding her shoes. She walks into a diner.

I park. I follow. I bring my wallet.

When I find her sitting in a booth she's speaking to a waitress. The seat towers over her head and she looks incredibly small. It makes me feel suddenly protective of her. These are the moments I like—when I see her and am genuinely sympathetic, when I see her and want to help her. It reminds me that there was a time when I was capable of loving someone. Letta sees me and she stops talking to the waitress and says, "I ordered blueberry pancakes. I hope you have your wallet." She smiles at the waitress and says, "That's all. Thank you so much," and she bats her black lashes. My maternal instinct disappears. I want to abandon her. Don't some species eat their young?

She has been crying, I think. Her lashes seem wet.

"I'm famished," she says.

"You're complicated," I say.

"I've seen a whole lot," she says.

"What have you seen?"

She laughs. "My dad's a coach. I've seen lots of games. Have you?"

"What grade are you in again?" I ask. I hated when adults did this to me, made me feel young.

"I'm a junior," she says, "but I'm so older than you."

Should I tell her what I've seen? I don't tell anyone what I've seen. My boyfriend and his best friend were killed in a car accident two and a half years ago on the road I live on, the long road, serpentine and lightless. It happened on the bend right before our house. We had been together for seven years. We knew I was pregnant and decided to get married, shotgun style, but when he died he died as my boyfriend. For some reason, people didn't see this as being as tragic, or that I deserved to grieve as much as, say, a wife. It didn't count somehow. We didn't tell anyone about the baby or our marriage plans. We were going to surprise our family and friends. We were going to announce it at our engagement party later that month. After he died I told a friend we were going to get married and she said, "Of course. Of course you were."

I've changed since then. Crème brûlée was his favorite dessert. I feel like the top of that dessert, a hardened shell covering goodness. I used to be happy. I used to love our home high on the hill, the sounds of the rain forest, its loud quiet.

He taught poetry at the college at the bottom of the hill. He said that if you teach poetry workshops in Hawaii, you would only read two poems. One poem will laud the spirits and the scents of the islands, and define the many meanings of *aloha*. For good measure, it will be laced with Hawaiian words: *pua* (flower), *aina* (the land), *makai* (the ocean). The other poem will be an activist poem. This poem will mourn the loss of Hawaii's *puas, ainas, makais,* and *aloha*. This poem will often curse the *haole*, a.k.a., whitey, "a.k.a., me," he said.

Once he came home and told me about a student's first submission. The student's name was Makaena. He read the poem aloud:

Go home, haole.
Once we had our own books

Our own words
Our own trees.
But you came and called us stupid,
And wiped us out with disease.
You made us wear clothes, made our women wear
      bonnets
Put an end to our chants and hulas, and made us read
      sonnets.
Auwe, I despise you, haole
You teacher, you preacher
Shall I compare thee to a summer's day?
Hell no.

He said that when he asked for a volunteer to read and Makaena said the title of his poem was "Compared to a Summer's Day," he had great hopes for the semester. He said that after Makaena read the poem, the girls cheered and the boys pounded a fist over their hearts and said, "Word."

I still have the poem. I read it and laugh because it was something that made him laugh and I envision him laughing. Makaena became his favorite student.

When the pancakes arrive I notice the waitress has a bruise on her neck. Letta has obviously noticed it as well because she's staring at it. I wonder if her mouth were to water would it be for the pancakes, or for the bruise on the waitress's neck. We both desire it—its proof of pain.

It's a strange reward, a dark secret surfacing, something you can show. I have nothing to show.

"Want some?" Letta asks.

I look at her meal—black blueberries on tan, immaculate cakes.

I shake my head. "No."

She's in the front seat now. She looks fragile. I imagine this is what it's like having a child—they don't apologize or say thank you, but when they come to the front seat you feel grateful.

"That party tonight was beautiful," she says.

We are on the road that winds up to our homes. The long road that's full of curves. A lot of people die on our road. There are wooden crosses, dried flowers and leis, stuffed animals and cans of food marking people's places of death. If he were to talk to me from the grave he'd joke, "Where's my stuff? I want crème brûlée on the side of the road. I want pictures of myself, my students' poems. I want a maile lei." But I know that really he wouldn't want anything. It's what other people do. People like the Kealanas. People like Letta's father's friends.

"I can't believe I kissed that guy," she says. "I just wanted to feel good. If that makes sense."

"I'm sorry," I say. "Doesn't make a whole lot of sense." But, of course, it does. Perfect sense.

"If I see that guy ten years from now, he won't remember what we talked about, but he'll remember that we kissed at a luau for a dead baby."

"There are other things to be remembered for," I say.

"In twenty years, if we bump into each other somewhere, what will you remember me for?" she asks.

I don't answer. I could be her stepmother one day. Who knows? How would I be remembered? As the woman who lived next door. The neighbor who could have helped, but instead made life worse. The Gold Coast specialist. What was her name?

There are signs along the side of the road—POINT OF INTEREST 2 MILES, POINT OF INTEREST 1 MILE, SCENIC ROUTE BEGIN. I see brown, withered ginger leis hanging from a guardrail.

"My spontaneity," Letta says. "You'll remember me for that." She reaches over me and turns off my headlights. I keep them off, but slow down and squint to see the lightless road. I tighten my grip on the steering wheel and scoot closer to the windshield.

Letta says, "I feel like he's here with us now. The baby."

"Don't say that," I say.

"Why not?" she says. "I can feel him."

"You know—some nights, you're not supposed to smile and laugh, or run into traffic. There should be no dancing, no kissing, no turning off headlights and lightly ruminating over a dead child. Stop making heavy things light."

"You don't understand," Letta says.

"What do you mean? I have to live in Waianae or something to understand grief or death? I have to be seventeen? I have to have a sick mother?" I shouldn't have said that. "You bring out the worst in me," I say.

"Your panty hose brings out the worst in you," she mumbles. "Will you stop? Stop at the lookout."

"No," I say.

"You have to!" she yells. "Please. Please just pull over."

Her voice is so desperate I can't resist. I drive into the lookout that hovers over Manoa Valley and a cluster of Honolulu city lights.

"What are we doing?" I ask, looking around. There are other vehicles parked—a black truck and a small, revamped Japanese car. The car is tricked out with glinting rims, rear spoilers, a body that's lower than it should be, so that it says *I am young and cool and getting some.*

"We're taking in the sights," Letta says. "We're ruminating heavily. Why do people need a view to get it on?" she asks. "Why don't they just park in an alley? Do you want to make out?"

"Good God, Letta. Make up your mind. Are you upset or are you a provocative, spoiled brat? Do you need a friend, a role model, or do you just need someone to rile and annoy?"

"I need someone to tell someone something for me," she says.

"What?"

She sighs, as if I'm incredibly slow. "I got dumped,"

she explains. "That's why I'm all upset tonight and why I kissed Kai. Anyway, this guy on my dad's team dumped me." She looks outside and I wonder if she's going to cry. "He's good at rebounds," she says, "but can't shoot free throws—he's like Shaq. He's my dad's pet. He has a tattoo of the Nike swoosh on his shoulder. He pulled a fuck and run. Dick. I was totally into him. I even did a reverse cowboy on him."

"What's that?"

"It's when you're on top, but you face the other way. You face his feet. He had huge fuckin' feet."

"Jesus, Letta."

"So maybe you could say something to him," she says.

I laugh. "Like what? What would I say?"

"Well, he totally used me, and I'm underage. I'm totally vulnerable. He's practically a rapist."

I try to navigate this territory as safely as I can. "But he's not a rapist," I say.

"Just an asshole," she says. "But still. He has a girlfriend, I guess. He said he loved her and that he made a huge mistake. Thanks a lot, dick. He didn't seem to love her when Annie frickin' Oakley was on his jock."

She rolls her window down and a scent floats into the car, the smell of dirt and plants. She turns to face me. "My father cheats on my mom while she's dying. He cheats on her with women who have huge breasts and working muscles. He cheats on her with women who don't have trouble breathing. Or swallowing." She looks at me in a way that seems accusatory.

I wipe some wetness from my eyes and am startled by the wetness.

"He brings them home," Letta says. "The latest one sneaks in at night, but I hear her. She thinks she's getting away with something."

"Who is she?" I ask. She gives me no sign, no clue.

"She's someone who doesn't mind degrading herself. She's someone who must know that my father doesn't love her."

"You shouldn't concern yourself with those things," I say.

"You shouldn't do those things," she says.

I look at the steering wheel and remain absolutely still.

"His name is Derek," she says. "The guy that dumped me. I want you to tell him that what he did was wrong."

So she has known all along. Now she's looking for payback. I'm trapped.

"When am I supposed to tell him this?" I ask.

"Right now," she says. "He's in the red car, making out with that girl. I knew he'd be here."

She sees my incredulous expression and before I can protest she says, "You owe me."

And she's right. I do owe her. I'm not sure what I'm supposed to say to this boy, but after I get used to the fact that I'll have to say something, I see it as a kind of opportunity. This is my chance to be good to her. I also see that I'm doing something that her parents don't ever do for her—protect her. It's so basic. She needs an adult to defend her, to help her.

I get out of the car. I step over the guardrail and look toward the back of the valley, then follow the dark tangled land down to the sea. The pickup truck leaves and I look over at the other car, prepared to see some kid's ass in the window, some naughty secret loving or impatient dry-humping. I walk over and as I get closer I see a couple in the front seat leaning over the console. It's dark but I can see them kissing. Gently. I watch as the boy brings a hand up to the girl's face, cupping her cheek, and I recognize the tenderness. It's something I haven't had in a while. It's something I don't ever want again. I watch these two. She's wearing his jacket, good God, letting everyone know she belongs to someone. A jacket, a diamond ring, a baby. It's as if our love never even breathed, never existed.

I pick up a few pebbles and throw them at the driver's-side window. They stop kissing. They look at my parked car. They don't see me on the other side of the rail blending in with the thick plants and uncut grass. I've ruined their moment. Or else improved it. Who knows? Now they're afraid. Now they'll kiss desperately.

I walk to his car and tap on his window. He looks at me angrily, then rolls the window down. He's much too big for the car. His knees almost hit his chin. I try to get a glimpse of his feet.

"Are you lost?" he asks. I'm surprised by his soft voice. I was prepared for him to yell at me.

"A little," I say. I don't know what to do. He clearly loves this girl next to him. Letta was a mistake. "I'm sorry to bother you," I say, "but I recognized you. I was wondering if I could have your autograph?"

"Oh, hell, ya," he says. He nudges his girlfriend. "A fan," he says. He opens the glove compartment without reaching for it and pulls out a pen and a yellow receipt for an oil change.

"I'll spell my name for you," I say. "It's difficult." I reach for the pen and paper and on the receipt I write, *Letta. You made a sad girl sadder.* I hand the pen and paper back to him. He reads it and looks toward my car. He scribbles something very quickly, looks at his girlfriend, who's going through her purse, then hands the paper to me. His expression seems to be asking me permission for something. I nod and the window goes up, then he starts the car and leaves.

Hi," Letta says when I return. She is playing with two rubber bands.

"Hello," I say.

When I sit down she leans over the console and touches my head, separating my hair into two sections. Then she gathers each section and fastens them into pigtails with the rubber bands. She has a gentle touch.

"There," she says.

I touch the two bunches of hair like bouquets on either side of my shoulders. It's funny how situating your hair this way seems to immediately transform you. It's as if the rubber bands recapture a lost child, a lost girl.

I hand her the piece of paper. She reads it and says, "That's fine."

It makes me sad that it takes so little to placate her. I read the note before I got to the car. It said, *I'm very sorry*, and then lower on the receipt he had signed his name and his jersey number. He really thought I wanted his autograph. This makes me smile, but I have no one to share my amusement with.

"My mother draws with her left hand now," Letta says.

"I know," I say, and just like that, something seems to settle between us, something has been concluded, quickly, like a slap to the face. "Why does she live in the studio?" I ask, envisioning this woman. I always picture her as being old, with a thick voice and a sharp stare.

"She didn't expect to live so long," she says, though this doesn't answer my question.

It does make me think of people coming to my apartments. I wonder if sometimes they're not just looking for the perfect place to live, but for the perfect place to die. Maybe that's when you know you're truly home— when you find a location you see yourself dying in. This road isn't the perfect location at all. It's always in shadow and you can never see what's around the bend. You can never truly know it.

"Can we go home?" Letta asks.

I like the way this sounds. It makes me happy to live

where I live: next to her. Tonight I loved and protected someone. Tonight I had a child. I start the car. I keep the headlights off.

I realize how ridiculous we look—two women coming home from a wake, driving without lights on, hair pulled into pigtails. A mongoose or a rat scurries across the road and I think of what Ronnie said—that Hawaii is the capital of endangered species. I imagine these species battling for the same land, learning each other's strengths, then adapting to obliterate the other. I wonder what Letta was like as a child. Before people and circumstances hurt her and she had to change.

We are almost home. Just one last bend. I don't know how I manage to make this curve every day. I see a flash of yellow from a reflector that was placed on the guardrail after the accident.

"So, I'll see you next Sunday?" I ask.

"Maybe," she says.

And that's that. She is done with me. I have served my purpose.

I take the turn. My eyes haven't adjusted to the darkness. I can only see splotches of things stamped along the road like mottled imprints of their original selves. I wonder if they're rocks or bushes, they could be anything in the lack of light—objects declaring love and loss, plants that recede in the sun, or endangered creatures stiffened by the sound of me.

The After Party

Sam's dad was once a world champion surfer, then a state senator, and most recently, a candidate for governor, a candidate who lost. It's been a week since the election and Sam can't figure it out, still dwells upon districts: Waialae, Waimanalo, Portlock, and Makaha, remembering that in each neighborhood where the family campaigned there were faces that beamed at the sight of his dad and cars that wore RIDE THE WAVE OF CHANGE, VOTE LLOYD SLATER on their rear bumpers. Sometimes he even caught people staring at his dad, openmouthed, as if he were a fire.

Sam had been looking forward to his dad's new title in hopes that more girls would like him, which was illogical because as a surfer's son they didn't like him, as a senator's son they didn't like him, so why would they like him as a governor's son? Sam can't surf. He can hardly paddle out to a break. Sam is semi-talented at playing the piano, an unfortunate semi-gift. He knows that girls don't care about the piano. They care about turntables and boys who are coordinated, and Sam's well aware that being uncool in Hawaii is like having a strange illness; you become an oddity, pitied yet quarantined like the lepers at Kalaupapa.

Sam sweeps the hardwood floors. He wipes down the side tables. He looks at the pictures his sister, his half sister, Bridget, has displayed. She likes to cut pictures from *National Geographic*, wolves, lions, slippery jaguars, and glue photos of family members' heads to the faces of the animals. Her collages are taped up along the wall, pictures of Sam and his family pawing and leaping, napping in trees, roaring in the Sahara. Bridget always makes herself the lion. Sam is always a prey animal, yet he doesn't mind prey animals. He likes their alertness, their dependence on the pack.

One of his dad's trophies weights down a photograph of his parents tandem-surfing. His mom sits on his dad's shoulders in a striped bikini. He holds her there easily as if she's slung on like a backpack. Sam looks at the gold trophy, the gold man on his gold board, the gold board on a golden, foaming wave. The etched honor:

World Cup
Lloyd Slater, First Place
December 5, 1974 Waimea, Hawaii

He imagines his dad receiving it, the crowd cheering, women throwing leis, and his dad at the center of everything, champagne in his hair, punching the gold man into the sky.

Sam moves into the kitchen to clean. He isn't surprised that his mother has flown to the Big Island without saying goodbye. The house is strikingly silent and still, as if someone important has just left or a party has just ended. The house is cold.

Bridget is sitting on a barstool, rubbing chocolate chips onto the granite of the kitchen island.

"Hey, Samantha?" she says.

"Yes, Gidget," he says.

She points to a chocolate smear. "Missed a spot."

"Why don't you help me out?" Sam asks. "They're your chores, too."

"I'm super busy," she says, lighting up a cigarette, then flicking a chocolate chip past him and into a potted maidenhair fern.

Sam ducks unnecessarily. His sister is free and angry and bitter about something. Apparently their family has wronged her somehow. Sam thinks it has to do with her real dad abandoning her when she was a baby. He can see how that could affect a person.

She's seventeen, only two years older than Sam, and yet she smokes cigarettes freely, gets out of chores unpunished, wins all arguments, surfs gracefully, and despite her cockiness is loved by all, or, at least, many. She's like a female version of Dad, Sam thinks as he wipes up her mess. And like him, she seems to know so much. Maybe she would have some answers.

"Why'd he lose?" Sam asks her, but quickly regrets the question. He doesn't want her to know how scared he is; how he thinks that if his dad falls they will all fall and with the way things are going this could be soon. This could be now. He's hoping his question won't make her laugh, or curse, or throw things. She glares at him, but then her face softens.

"Politics," she says. "Tricky stuff. I wouldn't take it personally. It's a party thing. Forty years, same party. Republicans don't fare too well here, obviously. Think post–Civil War South—that's how we were—dark-skinned laborers, white dudes on horses cracking whips. Think Mississippi in the fifties. That's how we are."

Sam doesn't know what he's supposed to think when he thinks of Mississippi in the fifties, and doesn't see what this has to do with his dad losing. He watches Bridget pick at the ends of her brown hair. She eats a chocolate then leans back and puts her legs in the air, balancing on the stool in a V. She takes a drag of her cigarette. "Working my abs," she says.

"Everyone seemed to like him," Sam says. "And Paul." Paul Strauss was his running mate, a POW held captive in Hanoi for six years. "It was so close," he says, wondering how much longer people felt they needed to remedy old wrongs. He wants to argue that Democrats in Hawaii are the new corrupt elitists, but knows it's not a fashionable thing to say, and he doesn't want to hear her defend his father's defeater.

"As I said. Tricky stuff. Lloyd should just switch sides." She returns to a normal seated position, her legs hard and ropy. "People think he'll infringe on their hula rights, I don't know. Fuck it. Anyway, can you imagine living at Washington Place? So gaudy. So nouveau riche, especially after Wailau's wife got her hands on it. Her colors are probably purple and white. The hedges are probably sculpted into balls."

"Mom could have changed that," he says.

"Mom can't change anything." She takes a chip off the counter, tosses it toward Sam, and he catches it in his mouth and feels proud.

"Good boy," Bridget says.

Sam hears his dad coming down the hall. He gets back to cleaning. Bridget gets back to smoking. His dad shuffles into the kitchen in tight exercise pants and hiking boots. He is shirtless. The hairs on his back are stiff and entwined like wedelia weeds.

"What a sight," Bridget says. "This is the legend we're supposed to love?"

He does look funny in his yard clothes, almost like a different person, but in his normal attire he's a handsome man, and Sam hopes that he, too, will be good-looking. He has the foundation for it—the dark thick hair, the height, the stalwart jaw and black eyes, yet so far the result is not the same. Sam's not as comfortable carrying his face the way his dad does.

"Don't go anywhere," his dad says. "It's family day."

Sam watches him slouch out the sliding glass door and around the pool to the shed. Soon he walks back onto the patio, leaf blower in hand. He pokes his head into the open door.

"Did Mom just go on a vacation, or what?" Sam asks.

"Christmas Bazaar," his dad says, then quickly revs up the blower. Brittle leaves storm into the clean kitchen, arcing back and forth. "It's family day, kids. Come help me in the yard."

"Super busy," Bridget yells. "Can't make it. Give my regrets to the grass."

When he leaves, Sam slams a bottle of cleaner onto the counter in front of his sister.

"Easy, pussycat," she says.

"The losses," Sam says. "Remember the losses. You promised Mom you wouldn't be such a bitch."

"Promises don't mean much in this clan. Now run along."

Sam walks to the shed to get the rake and a trash can. He can't understand where her anger comes from or why she refuses to see his dad as her own. One would think she'd have adjusted by now. He remembers that it wasn't always this way. His dad and Bridget used to dance together while he played piano with their mom sitting next to him as the page-turner. He played "Shiny Stockings," "Home Come'n," and "I'm Just Wild About Harry." Bridget was so light and little that his dad could flip her and swing her around his torso by her knees. He lifted her by her hipbones high over his head and sometimes she held a pose like a crescent moon above him. He probably could still lift her if she let him. Sam just wishes that for once she would put her cigarettes away and not have any opinions about anything. About politics, especially, but also about movies, books, fashion, and injustices done to people he has never even heard of. He wishes she would help him in the yard because their dad is having a hard time and a gesture from her would mean a lot to him. Sam can tell he's suffering both physically and mentally. In addition to the election, a few months ago his dad lost a few toes. Lawn-mowing accident.

Sam follows the groan of the blower. He finds his dad alongside the house, a grin stamped onto his face. Sam knows he isn't smiling. He's in a deep grinlike squint, as he always is when he does yardwork. Sam rakes the leaves into piles. He fills his bag with smashed putrid mangoes. The sun screams into his dark hair. He thinks of his mom on the outer island prowling the boutiques for her Christmas Bazaar, a huge event held at the house whose proceeds go to women's shelters. In previous years, his mother always shopped for the bazaar the first weekend of December and she had always taken Bridget. Everything is changing, he thinks. He isn't looking forward to the event, to helping, setting up, putting away, smiling. He's so tired of charities, fundraisers and parties, the leftover food and flowers, the excess, the not needed, the remaining.

Bridget takes the rake from his hand.

"Hey, there," Sam says. She has put on a wide-brimmed gardening hat and black sunglasses. She looks like their mother, pretty and slightly dangerous.

She walks toward his dad. "Hey, Lloyd!"

His dad looks up, turning off the blower. Sam knows he doesn't like it when she calls him by his name, thinks it makes him sound like the help, wants her to call him Dad, or, he jokes, The King, so Bridget sometimes compromises and calls him The Lloyd.

"What do you want us to do?" she asks, pained.

Sam expects him to turn the blower back on and point it at her face then laugh and hoot at the sky. Their relationship is one of brazen remarks and one-uppers, but he just points at piles, grunting through his stuck grin. "Here," he says, handing Sam a garbage bag even though he has one. "Hack off anything that's yellow." He walks toward the house, leaving the blower on the ground.

"Where are you going?" Bridget asks.

"My foot. It's hurting." He says this as if the pain of severed toes is a curious thing. "You kids go on. You don't need to do this. We'll do it another time."

"I can rent you a movie," Bridget yells. "Lawn-Mower Man."

"Shut up," Sam says. "Leave him alone," but his dad laughs.

"Good one," he calls back to Bridget.

Millions of leaves flap weakly at Sam: drooping teas, unraveling palms, languishing life on the breadfruit tree, a lame bouquet of tired things. "He's exhausted," Sam says. "Let's just do this without him, let's do the entire yard and not give him any grief, okay? We'll surprise him. It will be fun."

"Yeah, fun like dick cancer." She drops the rake. "We need shears."

Sam knows she's right. They aren't strong enough to just tug the leaves off as he's seen his dad do in one quick stroke. He doesn't like the stunned expression his father has recently assumed, or the way he seems to be dragging his body versus occupying it. Yet he's heartened by the fact that in public, his expression changes. He puts on his sharp face, commands his body. Sam wonders which face his dad prefers. He gets the shears and walks with his shockingly cooperative sister around the perimeter of the lower yard on the lookout for anything dying. Sam is also on the lookout for his dad's lost toes, even though he knows they're in shreds, part of the soil by now, reincarnated as mushrooms.

At the small dinner party last night, Sam listened as the alert and gregarious version of his dad told the story of how he slipped while mowing the yard, his foot sliding under the blade of the mower. Sam loved hearing it, loved the way he spoke to his friends. He resembled a man who had won. He told the story for a woman named Karen who hadn't heard it yet. Yet even Lana and Scott, who had heard the story, watched him carefully as if they were hunters, he the prized catch, full of promise and meat.

"So I'm sitting there, using my shirt to soak up the blood, and at this point I think I've been severely cut." His dad paused and looked down, shaking his head. He looked up again and snorted. "It was a little more than a cut, gang. Three of my toes were gone." He chopped at the air three times. "Gone. Off to the market. Wee frickin' wee all the way home."

Karen laughed, a little late, and cried, "This little piggy!" and his dad smiled at her with that arresting, sly grin Sam always tried to emulate.

"Okay. Then," he said, "I had to drive myself to the hospital 'cause these kids here ditched on family day and took off for the beach." His dad shook his finger at Bridget.

Sam noticed his sister was smiling, truly enjoying his father like everyone else was, but then quickly looked bored and slashed her finger through the flame of a candle.

His dad explained to Karen that he had to hold his hand down on the horn the whole time he was driving. "As a siren," he said. "Like this." He slammed his palm out into the air. "Beep beep!"

Sam watched Karen. He noticed that sometimes she would mouth the words his dad was speaking.

"Plus," he boomed, "I had to hustle because I was beginning to faint."

"Oh. My. God," Karen said.

Sam looked down and saw her toes squirming in her sandals.

"Here I am, blaring through traffic, swerving like a drunk, bleeding like a bastard, and my family's off at some beach!"

The guests shrieked as his dad acted like he was

slowly fainting, his beeping becoming weaker. Their shoulders sagged.

"So I finally get to the hospital and I know I'm going to pass out, so I put my head against the horn and, bam. I'm out cold. Hell of a ride."

His dad leaned back and drank his wine. Then he took off his shoe and showed his foot, extending it over the table, calling it "The Gimp," making the ladies scream. Scott teased him, said that now, when he's surfing, he would only be able to hang seven. His dad bellowed with laughter at this.

Sam eyed his dad's new, uneven foot, and knew that really the accident made him feel wobbly. He limped all the time now. Sam also noticed that he looked at his old surfing pictures a lot, which was understandable. Sam was proud of his dad's island fame. He was, after all, a surfing legend—one of the originals, one of the greats, a link to an older Hawaii, to Duke Kahanamoku and old Waikiki, to heavy wooden boards with no leashes, to big waves and slow styles.

Sam wondered what it felt like to win, to conquer something so large—to be a world champion, gashing the face of a twenty-foot wave, or to speak and have people mouth your words.

You do the leaves," Bridget says. "I'm going to mow."

"That's so unfair," Sam says.

"What are you, twelve? You're lucky I'm out here at all."

"Why are you out here?"

"I need a tan. Look at me." She extends the under-side of her arms. "Whiter than sunscreen." She puts her arm against Sam's. "You're just as bad. We're not true island children. We're imposters." She goes to get the tractor. The mower has been thrown away. She calls back, "I'll do the front and you can do the back."

Good deal, Sam thinks, and sees that it truly is a good deal. This is a gesture from her.

He begins with the yellowing teas and banana leaves. He saves the easiest part for last—the browning ginger and the tiare flowers—all he has to do with them is pluck. Sam sees Bridget on the tractor heading to the side yard below the monkeypod tree. She rides circles, carving large ones at first then making her way to the center. Sam watches her move past the circular drive-way, through the electric gate, and mow the strip of yard between their rock wall and the road. All he sees is her straw hat behind the wall, moving back and forth like a cursor in a video game.

She appears again at the other side yard under the plumeria trees. The roots of the trees make it hard to maneuver the tractor, but he watches her play with speeds, then she rides down the small hill to the lower yard and it's his turn.

The lower yard is all yard—smooth and easy. Sam gets on the tractor and rides out the rows. He sits back and turns up the speed, looks up at the mountain range, then quickly looks away. The range is named Kona

Kahui Nui, which means "man's large testicles." Whenever he looks at the mountain he sees green genitalia, rolling and abundant, or, as Bridget jokes, a ballsy rain forest, a testy mountain.

When he has put everything away, he joins Bridget on the patio above the lower yard. He gazes out at its expanse and everything seems to be moving, rising and breathing. He notices the white ginger is coming along nicely with its petals flapped open, panting. Sam is dusty and sweaty and, in the humidity, knows he will never get dry. He hears music. Yanni: his dad's favorite. Bridget yells at him to turn it down, that he's ruining the landscape. His dad comes out showered and striking in slacks and a striped collared shirt.

"You look nice," Sam says.

"Got a hot date?" Bridget asks.

"Looks good," his dad says. "Wow. Hell of a job." He stands beside them with his hands on his hips, gazing. "Look at this place," he says.

Sam and Lloyd and Bridget look at the place. Bridget flicks at sweat along her hairline. His dad grins in the bright descending sun. "Sorry I didn't help out today. I'm just feeling a bit tired for some reason."

"Late night?" she asks.

"It's fine," Sam says. "We had fun, and Bridget needed a tan."

"Yeah, no shit," his dad says, ruffling her hair. She

cringes. "Oh, Bridge," his dad says. "Lighten up. You're too pretty to be such a grump."

Sam watches his sister give no response. He watches her just stare into the fading day. He wonders what winter would look like in their yard—a mainland winter, a Midwest winter. He imagines the leaves, smothered and torn, the snow trampling the grass, stomping out everything until spring, the break in the sky, the blossoming, the pushing on. He considers putting the dead leaves back. We need seasons, he thinks. His dad needs seasons; his sister needs them, too. Spring and hail, a little dying, a little budding, the works. Sam is ready now—the house and yard are immaculate and it's time to discuss the election, to ask questions, to talk about their family and what they will do now that his father has lost.

His dad tells them to get ready.

"For what?" Bridget asks.

"Family dinner."

"Oh, for fuck's sake," she says.

Sam sets the table. He'll wait until they sit down. Bridget gets the leftovers from the dinner last night: sashimi, sushi, coconut ribs, and pear gorgonzola salad. They sit outside.

His first question will be about Paul Strauss—how Paul feels about losing; this will allow his dad to let his own feelings seep in.

"Are you just eating salad?" Bridget asks with her mouth full of sashimi.

"I'm not that hungry tonight," his dad says.

Bridget shakes her head, laughs as if she knows something, eats on.

"How's school, guys?" his dad asks.

"Good," Sam says.

"Adjective," Bridget says.

"Any good teachers?"

"Salzman," Sam says. "He says he's sorry you didn't win." Mr. Salzman never said he was sorry.

"You always ask about our teachers. You should listen more often," Bridget says.

He grins and nods. "That's right," he says, looking at his plate. "Did you hear that, Sam? It's good political advice. I need to listen."

"It wasn't meant to relate to politics in any way," she says.

Sam tries to think of something witty to say, or fun, because the conversation is taking on a bad tone, but he sits helpless, knowing that's another thing he lacks: comic timing. Quick humor. "How are you doing, Dad?" he asks.

"Oh, you know. Hanging in there. Hanging seven."

"It's unfair. The whole thing," Sam says.

"Not really," his dad says. "I did well. I paved the way for the next person."

"The next person?" Sam says. "That's unfair, too."

"Yup," his dad says. "It's how it goes. I'm going to have a glass of wine. You kids want one?"

"Please," Bridget says. "White." She points to the raw fish.

His dad comes back with a bottle and three glasses. Starts to pour.

Sam can't think of a question he wants to ask and it makes him angry considering he's planned all day for this moment. He watches Bridget and his dad eat contentedly as if their lives aren't ruined. When his dad is done eating he turns to face the mountain. The yard is dark now, muted and wet from humidity. Sam thinks he can hear it growing.

"Remember you used to put your napkin on your head instead of your lap?" His dad says this to the mountain.

"Yeah," Bridget says.

Sam thinks she is trying not to smile.

"Why'd I do that?" Bridget says.

"Probably just to tick me off."

"Probably to get attention," Sam says.

"What's wrong with that?" she says.

"Nothing, gang. There is definitely nothing wrong with that." His dad pours himself another glass of wine. Sam does, too. It makes him sink into his chair. Frogs begin to come up from their damp places and burp toward the gleaming pool.

"Look at them," his dad says, standing.

Sam looks at them, the wet frogs.

"Well, I'm beat," he says. "Going to bed. You can just leave the dishes."

Sam rolls his eyes, is about to say, "Yeah, right," but sees that he isn't joking; that today, no matter how hard he tries to clean up and air out, his dad is content to leave things as they are: a mess.

His dad stands there a while longer looking at the vanishing yard. "Top shape," he says then walks toward the house, taking his glass with him.

"Hey, Lloyd," Bridget says, and he turns back to face them.

"Yes, boss?" he says.

"You know the story you tell about your toes?"

His dad looks weary, impatient.

"We weren't at the beach. We were all at Sam's recital. He was pretty good."

Sam is embarrassed. "It's too complicated to explain all that. Jeez, Gidget, it's called storytelling. You improvise a little. It's no big deal."

"It's lying, Samantha. It's politics. All of this is a lie. We all don't even like each other." She looks at his dad, challenging him.

"I'll tell it right next time," he says. "You know me, always exaggerating."

"Can you clear something else up?" she asks, and Sam wishes that the night would swallow him. It's loud all of a sudden—leaves murmuring, fruit dropping. Sam realizes he doesn't want his family to talk to one another after all. His dad doesn't answer, just sighs and looks at his watch.

"Why are you so dressed up?" she asks. "Where are you going? You can't be going to bed. It's seven o'clock."

He shakes his head. "Leave it alone, Bridget."

"No," she says. "Are you going to bed? Look us in the eye and tell us you're going to bed."

His dad finishes his glass of wine. He looks at Sam, then at Bridget. "I'm going to make a phone call," he says, "and then I'm going to open another bottle. Give me two seconds." He walks away, leaving the sliding doors open. Sam worries that the frogs and mosquitoes will get in.

"What was that for?" he asks.

"He's going out, or he was, at least."

"So what?"

"He was going to meet that stupid chick who was over here last night. Not the first time. He has this fan club, you see—his *volunteers*. They all have cropped hair. They all have gumption and bright blue suits. He puts them in rotation. Mom found out. That's why she's gone. You're so stupid."

Sam wonders what she's doing. Why is she trying to tear their world down? Let him have his exaggerations, his fans. Without him they're nobody. Doesn't she know this? But he realizes how selfish his reaction is—he's thinking of the façade of his family collapsing versus the pain his mother must be experiencing if Bridget is telling the truth. He's thinking of public exposure versus private grief and his father's deceptiveness. He's thinking like a politician.

"You're just pissed he doesn't think of you as his real child," he says. "You're pissed at me because I'm the real thing." Saying this makes him feel small and young.

"Stop deluding yourself." Bridget's voice is delicate. Her eyes are watering. She does have weaknesses, he notices, and likes that she does.

"Mom should be here supporting him," he says. "She's gone because she's weak." Weak is possibly the worst adjective to describe their mother, but Sam can't stop—he has a compulsion to protect his dad, a willingness to look away. It's strange, instinctual.

Bridget lifts her glass. "Fine. Then cheers to us," she says. "To family day. Cheers to ending corruption, cutting taxes, strengthening military readiness, reforming Congress, staying united. To you, Sam. I'll play along for you. I'll focus on our family for you."

They are both silent. "I don't know what you want from me," he says, embarrassed by how he sounds, how both of them sound: adult and artificial.

"I don't want anything," she says. "Maybe I want you to admit you're wrong."

His dad reappears and Sam smiles at him. "We've settled everything. You can go if you want to."

His dad sits down and refills their glasses.

"Did you just get off the phone with Karen?" Bridget asks.

"Yes," his dad says.

"Well?" she asks.

"I talked to Mom, too. She's going to be away a while longer. She's taking a break. We're taking a break. What else do you want to know?" He leans back in his chair.

"Is she okay?" Sam asks.

"I don't know," he says.

"Are you guys splitting up?" Bridget asks.

"No," he says.

Sam detects desperation in her voice and remembers that Lloyd is the only father she has. She loves Lloyd and she hates loving him. She hates that everyone knows who they are. She loves that everyone knows who they are. He has a feeling that for his entire life, she will punish him for her confusion.

"Are you meeting Karen?" Sam asks.

"No," his dad says. "It was a mistake. Mom will be home soon. Everything will be fine."

They sit in silence, sipping their wine, swatting away the occasional mosquito.

"What are you going to do now?" Sam asks, taking advantage of the open forum. "For work?"

"For work?" Bridget says. "You just found out dad's boinking a young Republican and you're asking about work?"

His father seems irritated by the question. "KONA wants me to do a morning radio show, ESPN's doing a series commemorating Hawaiian sports. They want me to help with the surfing stuff. Lots of options. You know—this and that. I'll be fine, Sam."

The bubble of worries Sam has stored is suddenly, annoyingly popped. What a waste of time, Sam thinks, realizing how easy life seems to be for his father. One day, Sam can see himself inheriting this simplicity—he'll grow into his face, into his body, and will go forth easily into the world. He doesn't even have to understand the world. The realization doesn't console him. He looks at Bridget, the scowl twisting her mouth, her combative, bewildered eyes. She will have a difficult life, he thinks. She will understand the world. His sister, this quick and wise force, will always be much more lonely than him.

"So you were pretty good?" his dad says.

"What?" Sam says.

"At the recital. You were good?"

Bridget and Sam look at each other and don't answer.

"Why don't you play me something?" his dad says. "Since I missed out."

In the living room, Sam sits on the bench and places his hands on the yellowing ivory, eager to show his father what he's good at.

"No," Bridget says. "Introduce yourself and your piece and anything else you feel like saying. Be a fumbling artist."

Sam stands back up. "Hi, I'm Sam Slater and I don't know what I'm going to play, but that's just the way it goes."

"Good stuff," his dad says, and Sam smiles.

Bridget sits in the antique rocking chair their mom says is not meant to be sat upon.

Sam begins to play Bizet's First Nocturne in F Major, then stops because it sounds dull and he foresees a section he can't play well.

"Be a crazy pianist," his dad says, laughing somewhere behind him.

"Play that high and mighty furious thing you did at
your recital," Bridget says. "Pretend you're that cute
guy you have a poster of."

"Glenn Gould?"

"Yeah. Him. Play that pompous piece."

"Be victorious," his dad slurs. "Pretend you're on a
glassy wave."

Sam puts on a tortured expression and begins to play
Beethoven's *Emperor* Concerto. He tries to be furious
and passionate, wonders if he's managing to portray
even the slightest bit of brilliance. Or magnificence. He
thinks about his dad with another woman. He thinks of
James Bond and JFK, Hefner and Mozart, and all the
women who had been willing to pay for their license to
spy, govern, entertain. Why protect these men? What do
the women get? He imagines his mom alone in her hotel room and can't imagine her getting anything. Sam
turns to look back at his father, to gauge what he thinks
of his playing.

"Wait," Bridget says. "Don't move." Sam faces his
sheet music, seeing her move in the corner of his eye.
She goes to the stemware cabinet, opens a drawer, and
comes back with a red linen napkin and places it atop
Sam's head.

Why did she used to put a napkin on her head? His
sister has gone back to her chair and has shut her eyes.
Perhaps it was so she couldn't see. The napkin blocks his

vision like thick wild bangs. He can play blindly, so he does, closes his eyes and tears through.

"Nice," Bridget says, and she says it so quietly it's like a small draft cooling him, nudging him toward something.

He plays loudly because he doesn't have to be quiet and he has a lot of house to fill. When he finishes, Bridget claps and stomps her feet. He can smell the alcohol on his breath, the sourness.

He turns to see what his dad thinks and once again Bridget tells him to wait, to stop, but it's too late. He sees his dad sprawled on his back on the hard floor. This is the way he naps. He drops in random places like a sock slipped from a laundry basket. Once Sam saw him on the dog bed.

"He's tired," Bridget says.

"He got bored," Sam says.

"It was so nice, I almost fell asleep, too." Bridget looks as if she's about to cry. Her eyes are watery and soft. She was protecting him; a shot of instinct filled her as well.

"Don't be nice to me," Sam says. "You don't need to be nice." His voice trembles a bit. He clears his throat. "Besides, it's funny," he says, listening to the newly silent house. "It's funny. Everything. All of this." He laughs, but it sounds fake and bitter.

"Stop laughing, Sam," Bridget says. "I'm sorry he slept through that. I'm sorry we feel bad."

Her pain is undisguised and it frightens him.

"Why do you care now?" he says.

"Because I like you, dumb ass."

His father awakens. "Top shape," he says with a scratchy and frail voice.

"No, not really," Bridget says, and her sarcasm and coldness warm Sam. "Bad shape," she says. "Horrible shape. Ode to Sorrow."

"Keep playing," his dad says, as if he were never absent, sleeping and dreaming of glassy waves and women. He thinks I'm stupid, Sam thinks, but then realizes he's wrong. His dad doesn't think about him at all.

Sam continues his private concert with a simple, slower piece—something to give the night an agreeable sense of finality—but after playing for a while he decides to stop right before the climax, the part that's supposed to stir the heart, or some nerve in the brain.

He slams the keys with his palms. The inharmonious sound brings to mind someone falling, things breaking. "You've lost," Sam says. "You've lost everything. Even your toes." He stares at the keys for a while, then looks at his dad, who is pinching the bridge of his nose between his closed eyes.

"Yes," his dad says.

"You lost," Sam says.

"I lost," his dad says.

Sam wants to make sure his father knows that everything can't be conquered and ridden smoothly. He wants his father to see what he hasn't been able to do for an island, and for the even smaller island that is his family.

Bridget is looking at Sam in a way that suggests he has won something. He knows he has done what she wanted him to do: admit he was wrong about the person he one day wanted to be.

He wonders what his mother is doing. Perhaps she's on the hotel balcony looking at the other islands peeking out of the ocean in the distance, dark and still like half-sunken ships. They could all be having the same thoughts—his mother, father, sister, himself—the understanding that certain things are severed and they can't grow again, the sorrow that comes from loving a place that doesn't love you back.

Acknowledgments

I am grateful for the support of the Stanford Stegner Fellowship Program and the Richard Scowcroft Fellowhip. Also, thank you Scott Turow. I have been fortunate enough to learn from teachers whose work I greatly admire: Tobias Wolff, John L'Heureux, Dave McDonald, Elizabeth Tallent, Peter Cameron, and Sheila Kohler. Many thanks to Kim Witherspoon and David Forrer, Michael Ray and *Zoetrope: All-Story*, and M. M. Hayes and *StoryQuarterly*. One of the reasons Hawaii is compelling to me is that my family has made it so. Thank you for the gossip, the history, and the political and surfing lessons.

About the Author

Kaui Hart Hemmings was born and raised in Hawaii. She was a Richard Scowcroft Fellow in the Wallace Stegner Program at Stanford University and has degrees from Colorado College and Sarah Lawrence College. Stories from *House of Thieves* appear or will appear in *StoryQuarterly, Zoetrope: All-Story, The Best American Nonrequired Reading 2004,* and *The Best American New Voices 2006.*